WHICH OF THESE GIRLS...

WOULD YOU SPEND
YOUR TIME WITH?

"ENDE. IT'S A PLEASURE, TOUYA."

"MY NAME'S TOUYA. MOCHIZUKI TOUYA. WHAT'S YOURS?"

### Ende

A MONOCHROMATIC YOUNG MAN WITH WHITE HAIR, A WHITE SCARF, A BLACK JACKET AND BLACK PANTS. HE IS AN ENIGMATIC INDIVIDUAL WITH MANY MYSTERIES ABOUT HIM, ONE OF THEM BEING HIS ATTEMPTS TO USE COINS FROM AN ANCIENT ERA.

HE EXTENDED HIS HAND, AND I GRIPPED IT IN A FIRM HANDSHAKE. I REMEMBERED THINKING AT THE TIME HOW UNNATURALLY COLD HIS SKIN FELT. THAT WAS A FATEFUL DAY, THE EVENT THAT SERVED AS THE FIRST MEETING BETWEEN MYSELF AND THE BOY NAMED ENDE.

# In Another World With My Smartphone

Patora Fuyuhara
illustration · Eiji Usatsuka

IN ANOTHER WORLD WITH MY SMARTPHONE: VOLUME 3
by Patora Fuyuhara

Translated by Andrew Hodgson
Edited by DxS

Original Japanese edition published in 2015 by Hobby Japan
This English edition is published by arrangement with Hobby Japan, Tokyo

Find more books like this one at www.j-novel.club!

President and Publisher: Samuel Pinansky
Managing Editor: Aimee Zink

ISBN: 978-1-7183-5002-1
Printed in Korea
First Printing: April 2019
10 9 8 7 6 5 4 3 2 1

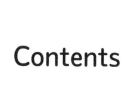

# Contents

# Simplified Map of the Divine Nation, Eashen

The Refreese Imperium

Bern,
The Imperial City

The Kingdom
of Belfast

Alephis,
The Royal Capital

Reflet

The Regulus
Empire

Gallaria,
Heart of the Empire

The Roadmare
Union

Yulong, Empire
of Heaven

Divine Nation
of Eashen

The
Kingdom
of Horn

The Ramish
Theocracy

The Holy
City, Isla

The Kingdom
of Felsen

Yulong,
Empire of
Heaven

Kawagoe

Dragon
Sea

Oedo

Ocean of
the End

Tsutsujigasaki

Divine Nation
of Eashen

The
Kingdom
of Horn

N

# The Story So Far!

Mochizuki Touya – a young man who died due to God's carelessness – ended up in another world. To make up for his mistake, God gave Touya a body housing unfathomable amounts of magic and a smartphone that could function in that world.

Using the powers given to him, Touya solved many problems and gained many dear friends along the way.

One day, by the request of Leen – a fairy he'd met in Mismede, the country of beastmen –Touya's group went to the Divine Nation of Eashen, which happened to be the homeland of Yae, one of his most trusted companions.

What awaited them in Eashen – a land so strikingly similar to Japan – was...

Before our adventure in Eashen began, we used a **[Gate]** to go back home to Belfast and properly prepare for the journey ahead. Our group consisted of Yae, Elze, Linze, Yumina, Kohaku, Leen, Paula, and me.

After we did all we had to in Belfast, we went to Eashen again and made Yae lead us through the dense forest. Shortly after I began to notice that the leaves were letting through more and more sunlight, the view before us became clear of foliage.

"Whoa…" I couldn't contain my voice. We were standing on a small hill, looking down at a large town with paddy fields surrounding it. There was even a castle. It wasn't a western style castle like in Belfast, though. It looked like the Japanese castles in Himeji or Osaka. Still, it looked somewhat small.

"That is my birthplace, Oedo, it is."

*Man, Oedo… sounds way close to Edo, the old name for Tokyo.* From a single glance, I could tell that the town wasn't really like the ones you'd see in historical dramas.

First of all, it was clearly a fortress town. There was a long moat and a tall stone wall to ward off any invaders. I could see sentries standing on the walls, and the turret towers built on them had archers inside. Some houses were scattered near the paddy fields surrounding the town, but most of the buildings were densely packed within the walls.

Eashen was by no means a large country. I heard it had an individual who could be called king, but he didn't get involved in politics too much, which allowed the local feudal lords to do as they pleased.

The nine lords governed their own areas, having disputes now and then, and with the king at the top, they had a somewhat functioning country.

*If I remember right, Yae said the names of the lords were Shimazu, Mori, Chosokabe, Hashiba, Oda, Takeda, Tokugawa, Uesugi, and Date... Okay, wait a second.*

The ridiculously familiar names almost made me think it was a joke.

*Is Eashen actually going through the Sengoku period? Are all the little states at war?* I tried asking Yae, and apparently, the country hadn't had any major conflicts for the past several decades.

*Probably a coincidence, I guess... Or is it...?* Yae's home, Oedo, was located in the east of Eashen. Tokugawa's domain, to be precise. From what I was told, he was a reasonably wealthy lord who was kind to his subjects.

"So, Leen, where are these ancient ruins you want to visit?" Though small when compared to many countries, Eashen was still a large landmass. We wouldn't find anything by searching aimlessly.

"I'm not sure. But I've heard the place is known as the 'Ruins of Nirya' to the locals."

"Yae, that ring any bells?"

"Nirya...? I feel like I might have heard that name before, I might... but I am not sure... My father should know more." For the time being, we just followed Yae into the town. Crossing the wooden bridge over the moat, we entered an area surrounded by walls.

Once inside the town, I couldn't help but notice just how Japanese everything looked. Most buildings were wooden, single-storied, and had tiled roofs. The entrances were shoji sliding doors, while shops had familiar curtain-style signs hanging in front. The language on them wasn't Japanese, though, naturally. The people passing by were clad in samurai gear or kimonos. Some looked like standard townsfolk, while others resembled casually-dressed ronin. Sadly, none of them had shaved foreheads or topknots. The most popular hairstyle was clearly the ponytail.

"Whoa, what's that? What are they carrying?" Elze was watching as two people walked across the road while hauling a kago, one of those carrier chairs.

"They're sedan chair bearers. You pay money, those guys lift you up in that chair and take you where you need to be. It's an alternative to horse-drawn carriages." Elze's eyes widened at my answer, and she stared at the kago as it passed us by. It wasn't a scene you'd see in Belfast, so it was probably a bit of a culture shock to her.

"Wh-Why do people have to be the ones doing the carrying? Carriages are far simpler and faster..." Linze couldn't have been more right. Honestly, I was sort of wondering the same thing. The only answer that came to my mind was "cultural differences"...

"The roads in Eashen are not as well developed as the roads in Belfast. It is highly troublesome to travel on them with carriages, it is. Horses are also scarcer here, they are."

*Well, that makes sense. I guess there are places in the world where services like this are the easiest solution.*

"Touya, that person there is wearing wooden shoes."

"Wooden shoes? Oh, those are called geta."

"Why is that bell hanging from that tower?" Linze questioned.

"That's the fire lookout's fire bell..."

"What a beautiful sound... What are they selling there?" Yumina inquired.

"Wind chimes. The wind blows and you just enjoy the sound..."

"...Touya-dono, despite not being born here, you have a strange knowledge of Eashen, you do."

*Well, I guess I know a little more about Japanese history than I should... My grandpa used to watch historical dramas with me all the time.*

Something didn't sit right with me about the town. The townspeople didn't seem all that happy. It was as if they were afraid or anxious about something...

Yae led us through a shrine's torii arch and a bamboo thicket road that took us to an open space, where we found a large residence surrounded by a fence.

We passed through a magnificent gate with a sign that said "Kokonoe Shinmei-style Swordfighting Dojo, Kuyoukan." Once we walked into the house's entrance hall, Yae raised her voice.

"Is anyone home?!" A few moments later, following some audible footsteps, a female servant with her hair neatly tied up behind her head came to greet us. She looked approximately twenty years old.

"Yes, hello. Greetings... Oh my, Yae-sama!"

"Ayane! It has been so long, it has!" Pleasantly surprised, the servant named "Ayane" ran up to Yae and took her hand.

"Welcome back, Yae-sama! Nanae-sama, your daughter has returned!" After she said that, another set of footsteps echoed through the halls. Moments later, we were joined by a mature, gentle-looking woman. She wore a purple kimono and looked like she was in her late thirties. I could see some resemblance to Yae in her features.

"Mother! I have returned!"

"Yae… I'm so glad you're alright… Welcome back." So she was her mother, just as I'd thought. Nanae embraced her daughter tightly. It must've been a long time since they'd seen one another. I could see some tears shining in her eyes.

"Yae, who are these people?"

"Ah, yes. These are my friends. They helped me get through a lot, they did."

"Oh my goodness… You have my sincerest gratitude for taking care of my daughter." Yae's mother sat on the floor and bowed her head. I was quick to tell her that she was overdoing it. It really shone a light on what a doting mother she was. Not everyone could express thanks with that position, even if it was related to their children.

"N-No need for that. We did as much for her as she did for us, so please, raise your head."

"Mother, where is Father? Did he go to the castle?" Nanae and Ayane looked at each other, gloomy expressions clouding their faces. Moments later, Nanae stood up and began slowly explaining the situation.

"Your father isn't here. He… went to battle alongside Lord Ieyahsu-sama."

"To battle?!" Yae raised her voice in surprise and stared at her mother.

*A battle, huh? That's pretty grim. I was under the impression that the king around here had things united.*

"Who are they fighting against?"

"Lord Takeda. A few days ago, he launched a surprise attack on the northwestern town of Katsunuma and is now advancing toward Kawagoe. To stop them, the master of the house and Jutaro-sama made their way to the fortress in Kawagoe." Instead of Nanae, the one to answer now was Ayane.

*So the lord of the neighboring territory suddenly began attacking this one, huh…?*

"Brother went with him, too…? I just do not understand… Why would Lord Takeda suddenly invade us like this…? I cannot imagine Lord Takeda Schingen ever allowing something so foolish…!"

"I hear that Lord Takeda recently hired a strange strategist to join his retinue. The man was named Yamamoto, I believe. The people say that he is a swarthy man with only one eye, that he uses mysterious magic… He might have somehow influenced Lord Takeda."

*Huh, Nanae's explanation doesn't really make any sense… Takeda's strategist. Yamamoto. That can only mean one guy. Yamamoto Kansuke. One of the "Twenty-Four Generals of Takeda Shingen." But Nanae's making him sound like some kind of weird wizard… Maybe it's not so smart to conflate this Kansuke with the one I've heard of… Even if they do share some similarities, they could still be pretty different.*

"So how is the battle going?" After listening quietly for a while, Leen suddenly spoke up. Paula, who was standing at her feet, slightly tilted her head to the side as well. Kohaku, who was sitting right next to Paula, saw that and did the exact same thing.

*Heh, cute. Wait, now's not the time for that.*

"Due to the surprising nature of the attack, there are rumors that our side could not gather enough soldiers. They say it is only a matter of time until the fortress in Kawagoe is conquered."

"But father and brother are there…!" Ayane's words filled Yae's face with dread. But just as quickly as that dread had appeared, it vanished and was replaced with a look of burning determination. We knew all too well that Yae wasn't one to sit still if her family was in danger.

"Touya-dono! I have been at a ridge not so far from the fortress at Kawagoe in the past! Please...!"

"Alright. Let's go."

"Thank you, Touya-dono!" I took Yae's hand and stated what I was about to do. Elze, Linze, and Yumina all nodded in agreement.

"I didn't expect to go to war. However, I can understand how she feels, so I'll come along as well." Leen shrugged and adopted a faint smile. Little Paula was fully up for it as well, expressing her intentions with a little shadow boxing. I didn't expect *that* to be in her programming.

"Yae, picture that ridge in your mind."

"Very well, I will." I took both of her hands, closed my eyes, and lightly pushed my forehead against hers. I wasn't embarrassed at all, which was a given considering the dire situation.

"**[Recall]**." I could see a certain scenery. There was a large, solitary cedar tree and a distant castle... No, it was a fortress. That was Kawagoe, no doubt about it.

I let go of Yae's hands and opened a **[Gate]** right there in the entrance hall. Yae was the first to dash through. The rest of the girls followed and disappeared moments after.

The sight left Nanae and Ayane staring in disbelief, so I took it upon myself to say something.

"We will do anything we can to bring Yae's father and brother back to you. I'll make sure we're all back in one piece, so don't worry."

"What *are* you...?" I couldn't think of a good answer to Nanae's question, so I laughed it off and ran through the **[Gate]**.

We stood on the ridge overlooking the fortress. It was clearly under assault, releasing black smoke into the sky.

I used the Null spell [**Long Sense**] to take a closer look at the situation. The hill fortress was somewhat holding back the invasion of the enemy forces, but the fires here and there made a portion of the defenders shift their focus on putting them out, which meant less men to repel the enemy.

The flaming arrows didn't stop, either. They continued to rain down as the incoming soldiers gathered around the walls and climbed up.

I took out my smartphone and run a search for "Yae's brother." *It isn't the first time I've ran a search for him, so it should work... There.* He was in the fortress, running back and forth along the walls. He didn't seem hurt, judging from his pace.

"Your brother seems fine for now. Don't know about your dad, though."

"We have to hurry inside...!"

"Hold it. Do you actually think you can just *walk* over and get in there?" Leen stopped Yae from recklessly charging toward the fortress. It was surrounded by the enemy, so getting inside was no easy task. But that didn't mean we were out of options entirely.

"I'll cast [**Long Sense**], survey the area one kilometer away, and use a [**Gate**] to get there. If I keep doing that, I'll be in the fortress in no time. I'll go alone first, so we don't get spotted. Once I get in the fortress, I'll open a [**Gate**] to connect you guys there, so wait for me here."

"I see. That does seem to be the safest route." Leen put her hand on her chin and began pondering something. *Oh, wait a second...*

"Hey uh... can't you fairies fly around with those wings on your backs?"

"Hm? Oh, no, it's impossible. Unlike the avians, our wings have devolved. We can flap them, but they only let us float for a brief moment. Not to mention that it's very tiring."

*That's a shame... It'd be easier if she could fly me above the fortress or something... Then again, the defenders might think that I was dangerous and try to shoot me down, so I guess it'd be a stupid thing to do regardless...*

Thus, I went with my original plan anyway.

"Kohaku, look after them. Contact me if something happens."

"Very well."

"What?! The tiger talks?!" Leen's eyes widened in surprise.

*Wait, didn't I tell you already...? Oh, right... it was supposed to be a secret since you're an important Mismedian... Well, she said she wouldn't tell anyone about my powers, so I'm sure she'll keep this one a secret too.*

I used **[Long Sense]** and looked one kilometer ahead. *Looks like a good spot...* I opened a **[Gate]** in a grove close to the fortress.

"Alright, I'm off." I stepped through the portal and came out in the grove. I could hear war cries and roars nearby, and the air felt downright unnatural. The abhorrent mix of fire and blood created a foul stench.

I looked up at the fortress and thought about what my next move should be. *Just two more teleportations could get me into the castle, but I'd rather get in without being spotted by the enemy.*

I cast **[Long Sense]** once again. And, sure enough, with all the soldiers surrounding it, there was no way for me to just warp in unnoticed. *No other options, then. I have to reach a spot with only a few enemies, take care of them, and then warp into the fortress...*

I looked for a place with a comparatively small amount of soldiers, but it took quite a few uses of my spell. Soon enough, I found a place not too far from the fortress' side. I could buy a lot of time after downing the two bowmen hanging around there.

"Reload." I inserted rubber bullets imbued with [**Paralyze**] into the Remington New Model Army holstered on my right hip and actual bullets into my gunblade, Brunhild, which was hanging on my back. I had to be prepared in case they had any magic-warding amulets.

"[Gate]." Drawing my New Model Army, I opened a portal to a spot where the two enemies couldn't see me. From there, I took aim and fired paralyzing bullets at their backs. *This feels a bit cheap...*

They got hit and fell to the ground, but instead of getting paralyzed and staying that way, they slowly stood up and pulled out their katanas.

*What the hell?!* What surprised me wasn't the fact that they weren't paralyzed. It was their strange appearance.

Japanese-style armor on their bodies, helms on their heads, swords in hand — all of that was fine. But the masks covering their faces were absolutely weird.

They were oni masks. Red oni masks with horns and the angriest possible expression sculpted on them. Japanese headgear had mask-like visors that protected the wearer from facial damage, but these masks weren't like that at all. They were wearing oni masks, wearing the very visage of monsters. There was no two ways about it.

There was another unnatural thing about them. I could see some spots of skin through their damaged clothing and under their helms, and it was all as red as the mask. It was as though they were red onis themselves, wearing masks to hide the fact.

Spurred by how abnormal they were, I hastily put the gun with rubber bullets back into the holster and took out Brunhild. Then, I aimed at the legs of the nearest one and fired a few real bullets. I had to immobilize them. I really didn't want a murder on my conscience.

However, as if to show how much my sentiment didn't matter, the soldier shrugged off the attack and charged at me with his katana. *Oh, crap!*

"[Slip]!" The friction of the ground under his feet dropped to nil, causing him to lose his balance and slump to the ground. *Yeah! Good old [Slip] to the rescue!* I took the opportunity to step on his sword arm with my left leg and kick away his mask with the other. The mask shattered and the face beneath it was revealed. He was red, that much was for sure, but it was a standard human face nonetheless. The man suddenly stopped moving. *Ah crap, did I kick him too hard?*

*Wait… are they being controlled by the masks?!* I took out the New Model Army again and fired a rubber bullet into the other soldier as he prepared to charge me with his sword.

The impact from the hard rubber shot made the mask crack and neatly split in two. When it fell to the ground, the soldier fell along with it, collapsing like a puppet with its strings cut.

*So it is the masks…*

"What the hell were they, anyway…?" I closed in on the collapsed soldier.

*Ugh… it stinks. Wait… he's dead! Do these masks control corpses and make them fight or something?! Can you even do that?! Wait… the guy I shot in the leg barely even bled…* It made sense once I realized that they were already dead. They didn't have blood flowing through their veins.

"Controlling corpses… Like necromancers from video games?" *They don't seem like zombies, though. They move way too quickly for that. Being attacked by these guys could ruin anyone's day pretty fast…*

I had to hurry into the fortress and decide my next course of action based on the situation.

Using **[Long Sense]**, I took a look inside the fortress. I didn't want them to assume I was an enemy and attack me. Finding Yae's brother and having him listen to me was the best option.

*Uhh… Oh, it has to be this guy. Black hair, black eyes, a slash scar on his right cheek, and he's wearing black armor. He looks pretty gentle, but he's gotta be some kinda battle god!* The man was encouraging his comrades, all while soaked in the blood of his foes.

**"[Gate]."** If I rushed in there, I'd run the risk of surprising them and making them attack me, so I kept the portal open a small distance away from the group. *There should already be a portal of light on their side… so I'll go in now.* I slowly crossed through and appeared before Yae's brother.

"Who are you?! Are you with Takeda?!" He readied his sword and asked for my identity. The soldiers surrounding him brandished their blades as well.

"Wait. I'm not your enemy. You're Kokonoe Jutaro, the brother of Kokonoe Yae, right?"

"Indeed, I am Jutaro… How do you know Yae?!" I raised my hands to express my lack of hostility. But Yae's name made Jutaro all the more alert. He glared at me with piercing eyes.

"I'm her friend. We met in the Kingdom of Belfast. We found out that you were in trouble, so we came to help."

"You're with Yae?!"

"I am. She's close by, too. Can I bring her over with my teleportation spell?" The soldiers surrounding Jutaro started to murmur, looking at the man as if asking what to do next. From the way they reacted to the idea of Yae arriving, I assumed they were followers of the dojo.

Soon enough, Jutaro lowered his blade and nodded slightly.

"[Gate]." A girl quickly jumped through the newly-opened portal of light. She looked around, noticed Jutaro, and ran to him at full speed.

"Brother!"

"Yae…? Is it really you?"

"It is!" As the two siblings had their heartfelt reunion, Elze and the others followed her through the portal.

"And they are?"

"My dear friends. They are reliable and kind people, they are." Being introduced like that made me feel a little bashful.

"Where is father? Is he safe?"

"Yes, there's no need to worry about him. He is currently protecting Ieyahsu-sama. You can see him later." *Ah… an elder brother gently talking to his worried younger sister. What a nice scene. But man… this is pretty grim.*

I looked around and saw a number of wounded people scattered around, they were clearly unable to move. Some of their wounds could've been deadly. *Alright, this is probably my best opportunity to try this out.*

I took out my smartphone and turned it on. The map app was already enchanted with [Multiple], so all that was left was the [Program].

"Begin [Program]／Starting Condition: A target on screen is touched／Upon Target Touch: Use [Multiple] to mark every matching target／End [Program.]" *With this, I won't have to bother locking on to every individual target. A single touch should be enough.*

Searching for just 'injured soldiers' would also mark the injured enemies, so I ran a search for 'injured Tokugawa soldiers.' Pins began dropping on the screen, indicating all the relevant targets. There were more than I had expected. I zoomed out the map so the entire fortress was visible on the screen.

I locked on to a single target by touching it, which caused all the other targets on the screen to be marked as well. I looked to my side and saw a small magic circle hanging above a writhing, injured soldier. It was the [**Multiple**] magic circle. *Alrighty, preparations complete.*

**"Come forth, Light! Soothing Comfort: [Cure Heal]!"** The magic circle began to spew forth some shining sparks. They covered the injured people below, causing each targeted individual's wounds to fade away.

Moments later, I could hear cheers from all around the castle. The injured soldiers in the room stood up and moved their bodies. They looked extremely confused.

"Wait… what did you do? I can tell that you used Healing magic, but did you actually…"

"I healed everyone in the fortress. Glad that actually worked, wow…" My words made Leen look at me like I was a weirdo. I could totally understand her sentiment.

"The injured are… What is happening…?"

"It's Touya-dono's healing magic, it is." Yae pointed toward me as her brother just stood there, wide-eyed and dumbfounded.

"It only closed their wounds, so don't have them do anything too taxing. Any blood they lost is still gone."

"V-Very well, I understand. I will make sure to notify them." Jutaro replied to me, but he still seemed to be dazed.

*Alright, that takes care of the injured. Now for the enemy attackers.*

"By the way, what are the oni mask-wearing things among the enemy forces?" I finally had a chance to ask about it.

"I am unsure. But I do know that until you break their masks, they do not stop moving even if you impale them with spears or lop off their arms. They are much like living corpses." He shook his head slowly as he spoke. *Oh, so I guess they're basically zombies after all...* I looked to the side and saw Leen leaning down on the fence, examining the masked soldiers. She was pondering again.

"Hm... It's either some Null magic... or an Artifact."

"Artifact? What's that?"

"It's a term for strange relics left behind by ancient civilizations, particularly ones that have powerful magic within them. I'm quite surprised you're unaware. Isn't that thing in your hand an Artifact?" She pointed at my smartphone, forcing me to talk myself out of the situation with a panicked smile on my face.

*Artifacts... So there's such a thing as ancient magic tools, eh? If there's some sort of controller that lets the user manipulate corpses, those masks would be like receivers, I guess.*

"Well, whatever the case, those masked things are troublesome. [**Paralyze**] doesn't work on them, so it's best to destroy them all in one go."

"...What did you just say?" As Jutaro gave me an inquisitive sidelong glance, I opened the smartphone's map app and ran a search for 'masked Takeda soldiers.' Pins dropped on the screen, pointing at all the masked soldiers around the fortress. I touched one of them, and all the rest were targeted at once.

"Wh-What is that...?" Someone whispered, so I looked up and noticed the veritable field of small, shining magic circles covering the sky. *Perfect...* [**Multiple**] *has them locked on.*

I raised my hand to the sky, focused my magic, spoke the spell, and unleashed hell upon my foes.

**"Strike true, Light! Sparkling Holy Lance: [Shining Javelin]!"** Spears of light burst forth from the magic circles, soaring toward their targets. It was as though light itself was raining from the sky. Mostly because light itself was, in fact, actually raining from the sky.

The earth began to rumble, clouds of dust were swept up from the ground, and errant sparks of light could be seen shining out from amidst the chaos. The cadence of the repeated attacks created a beautiful light show.

When the rain of light ceased, more than half of Takeda's army had been neutralized.

Then, I switched my search to 'Takeda soldiers' and locked on to them.

"Well, this won't be all that hard. [**Paralyze**]." The remaining soldiers, those that were fully human, suddenly jolted upright and then slumped to the ground. Some of them had magic-warding amulets, but the sorry state of their army made them set off fleeing.

"And that's the end of that." The Tokugawa army in the fortress stood there in silence for a good while, but once they processed what had happened, they all raised a roar of victory. I could hear cries of joy and relief mixing together and echoing throughout the halls.

"Did... Did you do all that...?" Jutaro turned to me. His voice was hoarse. He was looking at the area around the fortress, particularly at all the downed Takeda soldiers, clearly unable to believe what he was seeing.

"Well, I guess. I don't like being treated like a big deal, so I'd prefer it if you didn't talk about this too much."

"After all that we've seen from him, getting surprised is plain stupid." Elze put her hands on her hips and heaved a heavy sigh.

"I-It does seem a bit silly at this point." Linze agreed with her elder sister.

*Hrm... all I did was mix a couple of my abilities! Is it really that big of a deal?* I stared at the cheering soldiers, feeling a bit conflicted about the whole ordeal.

"Firstly, I would like to give you my purest of thanks for helping us with the battle." We gathered in the fortress' keep, which wasn't particularly large or fancy, and met a well-built man with a mustache. He looked to be in his early forties. The man sat at the seat of honor and bowed his head to me. Tokugawa Ieyahsu. The lord of this fortress and the territory it was built in. One of the nine lords of Eashen. I couldn't help but notice his name was "Ieyahsu," rather than the "Ieyasu" I was used to. The pronunciation was the same, but the spelling was different. I thought that was a little weird, but I could roll with it.

"Oh, we just happened to come around at the right time. No need to thank us." Yumina was seated in front of us, directly facing Ieyahsu. She introduced herself as the princess of Belfast, and us as her bodyguards. It was just a way to make the situation easier to understand, but I couldn't be more thankful for Yumina's social decorum.

Yae was counted amongst the "bodyguards," too. In short, we said that we came to help out because of our connection to her. Not like we were lying, either, so there were no problems to speak of.

"To think that Yae became one of Princess Yumina's bodyguards... Life is indeed full of surprises." Kokonoe Jubei suddenly spoke up. Yae's father was a large, grizzled-looking man who looked to be nearing fifty years old. Currently, he was the acting instructor of the Tokugawas. Due to his time instructing Viscount Swordrick's family, Jubei knew quite a lot about Belfast.

"Now... who is this youth that saved my fortress...?" Ieyahsu shifted his gaze past Yumina and directed it straight at me. *You're looking a little too inquisitive there, old man...*

"This is Mochizuki Touya, one of my bodyguards — or, as I prefer to put it, my future husband." Yumina's cheeks turned all rosy as she spoke. *Whoa, whoa, whoa! I did not consent to this! There was absolutely no need to say that!* The Lord and the instructor both sighed in a way that expressed both admiration and astonishment. I didn't like that reaction at all.

"Oh, I see now. The boy being betrothed to the princess of Belfast makes his feat easy to understand. How very splendid."

"Indeed. I'm very proud of him, too." Yumina puffed up with pride as though Ieyahsu's praise was meant for her. *Please stop. Please. I need an adult.*

"Praise aside, I would like to ask you a question... Have you heard of a place known as 'The Ruins of Nirya'? It's actually what we came to Eashen for..."

"Nirya…?" Yumina's question made Ieyahsu take a moment to think. Suddenly, something came to his mind and he lightly slapped his knee.

"Oho, you must mean the ruins said to house the secrets of Nirai Kanai. I don't know much about it, actually… What about you, Jubei?"

"From what I hear, the Ruins of Nirya are in Shimazu's territory. But they're supposedly at the bottom of the sea. Getting inside would be no trivial task…"

"The bottom of the sea?!" *What the hell? Is it some kind of water temple? Does it have an entrance that appears and disappears depending on the tide?! Well, not like we have any choice. We'll have to go see it for ourselves. Now we know where it is, so we can make our way there if we want… but the situation right now doesn't really give us a lot of wiggle room.*

"About Takeda's army… Do you think this will be enough for them to back down?" My question made Ieyahsu fold his arms. His head bobbed in thought.

"I believe they will regroup and try attacking us again. They may come with more of those masked warriors, perhaps even their cannon units…" *No amount of soldiers would change the result, though. Cannons might be troublesome, but I could still break them.*

"I must say, though… The masked soldiers, this invasion in general… it confuses me to no end. The Lord of Takeda, Schingen-dono, is indeed the proud leader of the four great military commanders known as 'Takeda's Elite Four,' but this battle felt rather unlike him. The rumors may be true after all…"

"Rumors?" Ieyahsu's words got me curious. Jubei spoke up to elaborate, rather than Ieyahsu himself.

"There are rumors that Schingen-dono might have already passed away. That his body is being controlled by a dark strategist known as Yamamoto Kansukay, who is using the shell of their Lord to lead Takeda's armies as if they were his own."

"Yamamoto Kansukay…"

"When you consider the existence of the masked soldiers, that doesn't seem impossible. He might have a spell or an Artifact that can take control of corpses." After listening to Jubei, Leen presented her own thoughts.

*Well, controlling that many corpses at once doesn't seem like a trivial thing to do. It seems possible to me. Does he plan on using Takeda to force all of Eashen to unite under one banner? Crap, now I'm thinking about Takeda's army. I can't exactly leave with a clear conscience now…*

"Would it all cool down if someone captured this Yamamoto Kansukay guy?"

"It might… However, Schingen-dono's death is nothing but a rumor. And, from what I hear, Kansukay never leaves Takeda's stronghold at Tsutsujigasaki. Sneaking inside and kidnapping him would be a fool's errand…"

*Hmph. That was exactly what I was planning, but I guess that does sound kinda silly, even if I could get in with* [**Long Sense**] *and* [**Gate**]. *It would be great if there was a spell that could make a person invisible, or… Ah.*

"Leen. You can use light magic to make your wings invisible, right? Is it possible to apply it to your whole body?"

"It is, yes. However, it simply makes the light encompass something, so people would quickly notice if you bumped into them."

*Alright… So she can actually make people invisible. That'll make the stealth portion easier.* I was already thinking of infiltrating the enemy fortress. So really, I'd prefer as few casualties as possible, regardless of friend or foe.

"A-Are you thinking of actually sneaking in?" Linze spoke as if she just read my mind. *Sheesh, is it that obvious?*

"If this Yamamoto Kansukay is really the mastermind, it'd be the easiest way to deal with the situation, right?"

"That's true, but…" She was probably worried about me, but I didn't feel that there was a need for that. I could always escape through a **[Gate]**, after all.

"The main problem is getting to this… Tsutsujigasaki place. Have you ever been there, Yae?"

"No, not even once, I have not. What about you, Father?"

"Same for myself… Why should that matter, though?"

"If we find someone who has been to Tsutsujigasaki, Touya-dono can use his magic to get there in mere moments, he can!"

"What…?!"

Jubei and Ieyahsu both looked at me in sheer surprise. I didn't really want to stand out so much, but since I was leaving Eashen after exploring the ruins anyway, I decided to just accept it.

"Allow me to be the one to introduce him to Tsutsujigasaki, then." A voice echoed throughout the keep, coming from seemingly nowhere. It didn't belong to anyone in the room. I quickly pulled out the New Model Army and aimed for where I'd heard the voice — out in the corridor surrounding the room.

"Who is there?" Someone took the words right out of my mouth. It was Jubei, who seemed as baffled as I was.

A person walked out of the shadows in the corner.

*Whoa, it's a ninja!* The black clothes were a clear giveaway. The outfit stood out, yet I still hadn't realized that the person was there, so it was possible they used some kind of perception-blocking spell.

The person took off the cloth covering her head, revealing the face of a beautiful woman. It was a female ninja. A kunoichi, to be more precise.

"I am Tsubaki, subordinate of one of Takeda's Elite Four — Kousaka Masanohbu-sama. I've brought a secret message to Tokugawa Ieyahsu-sama."

"You're with Kousaka-dono?!" The kunoichi kneeled on the floor, took out her message, placed it in front of her, and backed away. Even if the current battle was over, she was a ninja working for the opponent. It'd only be natural for us to be cautious around her. Eyes on the kunoichi at all times, Jubei took the message and handed it over to Ieyahsu.

I kept my gun trained on her, just in case. Better safe than sorry, after all.

Ieyahsu opened the scroll and began reading. A look of surprise dawned on his face, then he became sterner. *What could've made him react like that?*

"Milord. What does it say?"

"It seems that the rumors were true. Takeda's forces are naught but an army of puppets."

"It can't be…!" Jubei was at a loss for words. *So it's true. Yamamoto Kansukay had complete control of Takeda's army.*

"Schingen-dono has already passed away, and, with the exception of Kousaka-dono, Takeda's Elite Four are all imprisoned in the dungeons. The letter asks us to stop Kansukay and save the land of Takeda."

"Kousaka-sama pretends to be loyal to Kansukay. He's plotting how to take Takeda out of his hands in the shadows, however." The kunoichi, Tsubaki, gave us some more intel. According to her, Kansukay was hiding the fact that Schingen was dead. He used the corpse as a proxy to put the land of Takeda under his command. The Elite Four noticed. Three of them were imprisoned, but Kousaka pretended to be loyal to Kansukay and thus was spared.

"In all honesty, Tokugawa has no obligation to do so much for Takeda. But at this rate, the masked soldiers under Kansukay's command will ravage our lands. As pitiful as it might sound, the power to save both Tokugawa and Takeda lies in the hands of these Belfastian guests of mine." Ieyahsu looked at me. And with that, it became my duty to infiltrate Tsutsujigasaki and do something about Yamamoto Kansukay.

"What are you going to do, Touya?" Despite knowing the answer, Yumina went out of her way to look up at me and ask me that.

*So I'm the one who gets to decide the fates of two lands... Well, it doesn't really bother me.*

"Sure, I'll do it. I'll infiltrate Tsutsujigasaki. I want to go to the Ruins of Nirya with a clear conscience, after all."

"Thank you." Tsubaki bowed her head to me alongside her words of gratitude.

"Going in with a large group would be a bad idea, so the only ones to go will be me, Tsubaki, and Leen." Tsubaki knew the inner workings of Takeda and Leen was a fairy with great magic skill, so it was the best choice for a smooth operation. Sadly, Paula couldn't tag along this time. Once I told her that, the bear plush stomped on the floor in frustration and made her anger very clear. *That* [**Program**] *is damn impressive...*

"Alright, let's get to it and..."

"Wait, wait! Are you really gonna sneak in there in broad daylight? Shouldn't you wait for nightfall?" After I stood up and got ready to go, Elze said something extremely reasonable.

*Guess she's right... There'll be fewer people at night, and the darkness can help us hide. Even if Leen makes us invisible, night time is the better setting for a stealth mission.*

I decided to take a rest before the new plan. Well, it wasn't much of a rest. I had to use a **[Gate]** to inform Yae's mother that Jubei was fine, then teleport to Belfast and tell Laim that I wouldn't be back for the night, among other things. I even had to go to Oedo and buy alcohol, food, arrows, oil, and other things to resupply the fortress. With **[Storage]**, it wasn't tiring in the least, so I didn't really mind. Ieyahsu even gave me money for doing it. Quite a lot of money, in fact. A delivery service sounded more enticing than ever at that point.

The day went by quickly while I kept myself busy, and soon it was night time.

"Alright, Tsubaki, picture a place from which you can see the stronghold at Tsutsujigasaki. I'd be thankful if you picked a place that doesn't have many people."

"Understood." As Tsubaki closed her eyes, I took both of her hands. *Geez, I was tense enough doing this with Yae, but it's even more unnerving doing it with a stranger... Honestly, holding a girl's hand is heavy enough... so why are Yumina and the others glaring daggers at me?!* I had no idea what I did to deserve such glares, but I decided to get this over with. It felt like the safe thing to do.

"**[Recall]**." I focused my magic and pressed my forehead against hers. Tsubaki was about as tall as me, so I didn't have to lean in like I did with Yae. Soon enough, I saw the faint image of a big, single-story building surrounded by a few moats and a castle town. So that was Takeda's stronghold, Tsutsujigasaki.

"[Gate]." I distanced myself from Tsubaki, stood in the middle of the keep, and created a portal of light leading to the enemy stronghold.

"Okay, we're off. Kohaku, tell me if anything happens."

«Understood.» The tiger replied via telepathy. It was a handy little thing that allowed Kohaku and I to talk privately. If something happened here, Kohaku would tell me about it and I could get back in an instant.

First one to go through the [Gate] was Leen. She was followed by Tsubaki and then myself.

Once through, the first thing I noticed was the night sky. There was not a moon visible, but several stars twinkled in the sky. We were surrounded by a dense forest, and I could see some torches burning off in the distance. That was the Tsutsujigasaki stronghold, no doubt about it.

"So that's what we're infiltrating…" First, I decided to examine it using [Long Sense]. I could see some bridges built over the moats and, as I had expected, the gates were closed.

Guarding the gates stood some brawny fellows, clad in full armor and holding spears.

I looked beyond the gates and saw a long, white fence built sort of like a maze. Right next to it, there was a well. Not too far from there, in an open space, I saw a garden tree that seemed like a perfect hiding spot. *Alright, that's where we'll warp to…*

"[Gate]." I quickly opened a portal and tried going through. However… instead of letting me go through it like normal, it pushed me back after taking just one step.

"Huh?" I tried passing through again. But, just like the first time, I was repelled right after putting my leg in.

"What's going on?" I tilted my head in confusion. This had never happened before.

"A barrier talisman. That's the most likely thing that could stop you from going through the [**Gate**]."

"A barrier?" Leen came to that conclusion after watching me try a few times. I could recall Duke Ortlinde saying something similar, too. *Passage through teleportation can be stopped by the simplest of barriers... So that's how it works...*

"This is probably Kansukay's doing. I can go inside freely. I'm Kousaka-sama's subordinate, after all. Wait here while I destroy the talisman." As Tsubaki got ready to head into the stronghold, Leen folded her arms and stopped her.

"Don't. When you break a barrier, there's a high chance that the one who created it will notice. Even if they don't know that you were the one who did it, making them alert isn't a wise idea."

"What should we do, then?" There was only one possible answer to that question. Nothing else would work.

"Leen. Let's infiltrate the place with the magic that makes your wings disappear. You and I can become invisible, then we'll accompany Tsubaki as she passes through the gate. That should work, right?"

"It doesn't make them disappear, it just affects the vision and... Well, alright. Stand over there, then." I did as I was told. Leen placed her hand on me and gathered her magic, forming a magic circle beneath us.

**"Bend, O Light. Guiding Curvature: [Invisible]!"** After she spoke the spell, the magic circle rose up and surrounded us both. Once it reached the tops of our heads, it dispersed like nothing.

"You disappeared..." Tsubaki expressed her surprise.

*Oh? It's working already? But I can still see my arms, and the rest of me too! I can see Leen!*

"Leen. Is my vision unaffected by this spell or something?"

"Well obviously. Can you imagine how inconvenient it would be if you couldn't see your own body?"

"Oh, I can still hear you." Tsubaki sounded slightly relieved. *Wow, guess she really can't see us.*

Leen grinned, walked behind Tsubaki, and suddenly began fondling her breasts.

"Fhyaaaaahhh?!"

"Hey, Touya! Why are you taking advantage of her just because she can't see you?"

"T-Touya-san?! Wh-Why…?"

"It's not me! That's Leen! I'm still in front of you!" I moved the foliage around me to indicate my presence. *Heck, even if you can't see her, you should be able to tell based on the feeling on your back!*

"No… Ah, hey, that's… Ahh!"

"Hmm… They're unexpectedly big. Are you the type who looks slender in clothing? These are quite the melons…"

"Cut it out already!"

"Ouch!!!" Since she clearly wasn't going to stop the fondling, I hit her with a karate chop. *A 612-year-old has no business being this childish. Please consider the importance of our situation!* As Leen clutched her head and crouched down in pain, Tsubaki turned red from the embarrassment and backed away. Her arms were wrapped around her own chest. *Good job, Leen. You made our tenuously allied ninja friend wary of us.*

I spoke up, hoping to calm Tsubaki down.

"It's okay now, don't worry. I'll give her a good smack and make her stop it if she tries it again."

"...You're going to smack my ass?"

"Quiet, you!" Leen's joke made Tsubaki back away even further.

*Can we even succeed if it goes on like this?* I became slightly... No, I became very worried.

"I am Kousaka-sama's subordinate. Let me pass."

"I see. Just a moment, then." The two guards looked at Tsubaki's permit, nodded, and slowly opened the heavy gate. The place didn't seem to have a separate entrance for individual people.

Still invisible, Leen and I quickly slipped through the open gate as well. Tsubaki walked through a moment later and the guards closed the entrance once again. *Whew... We made it.*

"Hey, Leen. Shouldn't the barrier dispel our invisibility?"

"As a rule of thumb, barriers only repel magic that affect their area of influence. It won't dispel the spell on us because, instead of affecting the area, it affects only us. That's also why the barrier shouldn't prevent you from leaving through a **[Gate]**." That made sense to me. A **[Gate]** only affected the destination, after all. I couldn't enter, but I could leave with no problem. That was also why my **[Long Sense]** wasn't dispelled. The target of the spell wasn't the area, but me.

Anyway, now that we were inside, we had to go save the three members of the Elite Four who were locked up in the dungeons, then ferry them out with a **[Gate]**. Though if they were capable of fighting, I'd gladly have them join us. I suggested my idea to Tsubaki, who instantly agreed.

"The dungeon is this way." Following Tsubaki, we ran through the moonless night.

The dungeon was in a building near the west edge of the stronghold.

Tsubaki said that not even her permit would let her inside. I had Leen make her invisible like us and we all used our collective vanishness (according to Leen, that wasn't the right term, but whatever) to sneak inside.

We passed the guard room and walked down the stairs. In the dungeons made from stone and wood, I could see an old man. His eyes were closed and he was sitting in quiet meditation. The man was large in build, had long, graying hair and a face with several wrinkles here and there.

"Who is there?" Still meditating, he suddenly spoke up, surprising all three of us. He could sense our presence despite our invisibility, it seemed.

"Baba-sama, I'm Tsubaki. Kousaka-sama ordered me to help you. Do you happen to know where I could find Naito-sama and Yamagata-sama?"

"You're one of Kousaka's? Hmph, I had a feeling that he was only pretending to be part of Kansukay's army. He's not one to be underestimated." Clearly amused, one of Takeda's Elite Four, Baba Nohbuharu, bore a wide grin.

"Naito and Yamagata are in the cells further down. But don't you think you should show yourself first?" Leen canceled her spell, making Baba raise his eyebrow and stare at us.

"Who are these two? I don't recognize them."

"These are guests of Tokugawa-dono. Their names are Mochizuki-dono and Leen-dono. Mochizuki-dono is powerful. He defeated the fifteen thousand masked soldiers that attacked Tokugawa all by himself."

"He what?!" Old man Baba's eyes opened wide. *W-Wait… there were fifteen thousand of them?! I didn't know that! I guess that explains why the map app had so many pins on it…*

The old man was still looking at me in disbelief, but there were more important things to do than be awestruck. I could use magic to blow the cell open, but that would attract too much attention. Thus, I only had one course of action.

"**[Modeling]**." I changed the shape of the grating and began creating a space for a person to pass through. It took me about a minute to finish it, after which old man Baba walked out as if he was never locked up.

"I see that you can do some strange things, squirt."

*S-Squirt?! Well, I guess I am way younger than you…* I chose not to say it, but I could've easily brought up that the fairy with me was way older than him.

The rough old man joined us as we walked through the dungeon and reached two more cells. They were on opposite sides of the room.

The one on the right held a gentle-looking man who appeared so ordinary that I couldn't help but compare him to an office worker on the verge of retirement. The one on the left, however, held a middle-aged man with the eyes of a warrior and countless battle scars all over his body.

"Oh, Baba-dono. Glad to find you in good health." The office worker turned to us.

"Looks like things are getting interesting, Baba-dono. Lemme join, in case things get wild." The scarred man grinned with excitement, stood up, and walked over to the grating. Seeing the way they acted, old man Baba heaved a long sigh.

"Naito. How about taking this a bit more seriously, eh? The way you're always smiling like that really gets to me. And you, Yamagata. You should try using that noggin of yours every once in a while. Not all problems can be solved with battles." *Hmm... So the office worker was Naito Masatoyoh, and the scarred one was Yamagata Massakage.*

"Hey squirt, get these two out of their cells, will ya?"

"Fine by me. But could you stop calling me squirt? I have a name, and it's Mochizuki Touya." As I looked at and waited for him to correct himself, Leen joined the exchange.

"Just so you know, this boy is first in line for the throne of Belfast, so you ought to take care in how you talk to him." All three of the men were at a loss for words. *Well, she's not wrong, but that description still doesn't sit right with me... I still haven't agreed, after all.*

"Really, now? Hmm... But changing the way I call him would make me look pathetic at this point... Well, he'll just have to deal with being called squirt." Baba's response made Leen smile and shrug. *Well, shit. Guess he just doesn't listen to people.*

"I will take the liberty of calling him Touya-dono."

"Then he'll be Touya to me." Just like Baba, both Naito and Yamagata went with whatever they were comfortable with. *Man,*

*Takeda sure is full of people who act however they want. Shame that Schingen's dead. I would've loved to meet the guy who got this group of misfits to listen to him.*

I used [**Modeling**] to free the two men just like I'd freed old man Baba. Then, I got Leen to make us invisible and we all made our way through the guard post and out of the dungeon.

"What do we do now, Your Soon-to-be Majesty?" Naito spoke with a smile on his face, clearly making fun of me. *I do not approve of this, not at all.* I got everyone together and told them my plan.

"I intended to let you three escape the stronghold and go on to capture Yamamoto Kansukay with my group, but…"

"Hey now, we can't have that. Take me with you, Touya. We all have a score to settle with that bastard, you know?" Yamagata cracked his knuckles, a fearless smile spread across his face. With his face being so scarred, that motion was scary in more ways than one.

"Kansukay is surrounded by the oni mask soldiers, and he himself uses some strange magic. Guy's inhuman. Think you can really beat him?" Old man Baba said something strange. As my expression became a confused one, Naito continued where Baba left off.

"Yamamoto Kansukay was once a strategist under Schingen-sama's command. A capable man with a good head on his shoulders, he was an excellent strategist. But he somehow got his hands on a jewel imbued with demonic power. Ever since he got his hands on that, he seemed to get crazier every day. He began killing cats and dogs, started doing weird experiments… and that soon escalated to the point of him committing actual murder. Since then, he created the corpse-controlling 'oni masks' and became more powerful than ever. We couldn't stop him. The power in that jewel of his was far too great…"

*So, that thing actually made Yamamoto Kansukay go insane? Some kind of demonic power, huh? That was probably the Artifact controlling the corpses.*

"What do you think, Leen?"

"There's little doubt that this jewel made him lose his sanity. Artifacts might sometimes be so strong that they develop a mind of their own. They could even house such things as the grudges or obsessions of their creators." *Grudges...? That makes it sound like a cursed item.* Whatever the case, Leen made it easy to understand. Takeda's strategist, Yamamoto Kansukay, was being controlled and turned insane by a cursed jewel. Therefore, it was safe to assume that breaking the jewel would take care of the situation.

"So, where can we find Kansukay?" I turned to Tsubaki.

"I believe he might be in the building in the central quarter of the stronghold..."

I took out my smartphone and ran a search for 'Yamamoto Kansukay,' but didn't get any hits. *Hmm? Is he somewhere else? No, that can't be it.* To confirm my suspicions, I ran a search for 'Leen,' but didn't get any results either.

*It's that damn barrier. It's blocking my* [**Search**] *enchantment. Man, what a pain.*

"Tsubaki, where is the central quarter?"

"Uhm... It's in this direction." I used [**Long Sense**] to move my sight toward where she was pointing. It was a spell that affected me, so the barrier couldn't do anything about it.

Once I passed the large garden and was about to take a look inside the building, I saw a man walk out of it.

A black kimono, a black hakama, swarthy skin, and an eyepatch over the left eye. *That's Kansukay, no doubt about it.*

I took my sight back and asked Leen how to destroy the barrier. Since I already saved the Elite Four, all that was left was to prepare myself for the moment they found out. Then all I had to do was teleport to Kansukay.

"I believe there should be magic-imbued talismans placed at the four corners of this stronghold. Breaking just one of them should do the trick."

"I know where to find one. Follow me." We all followed after Yamagata. Thanks to our invisible forms, we got there without anyone noticing.

There was a small stone jizo statue placed in a little hole in the wall. It was about as tall as Paula.

"No doubt about it. This little jizo is one of the talismans."

A statuette? Not exactly the first thing that comes to mind when hearing the word "talisman." In this world, "talisman" seemed to share its meaning with "charm" and the like, so they came in many shapes and sizes.

"So, we should just break this and teleport straight to Kansukay, right?"

"Now wait just a second, squirt. We might be tough, but going in without weapons is crazy. Don'tcha have something for us?" *Sheesh, this guy sure is the demanding sort...* Old man Baba was completely right, though. But the only weapons I had on me were the New Model Army and my gunblade, Brunhild. Neither of them were something I could give to them...

"Well. Guess I'll have to make some."

"Make some?" The Elite Four looked at me like I was a lunatic. I ignored their stares and used [**Storage**] to take out the steel I kept from when I was making bikes.

"You okay with a spear? Do you have any requests or preferences?"

"Hm? Yeah, I'd like a spear. Naito does best with two short swords, and Yamagata likes his greatswords..."

"Sure thing." I used [**Modeling**] to reshape the steel. First, I made the two short swords. Then came the greatsword, and last, but not least, the spear. The three took their weapons and tested out how they felt and handled.

"To make something like this in such a short amount of time... You are amazing, Touya-dono."

"The whole thing's made of steel, so I thought this spear would be heavy... but it's surprisingly light. Balance is a little strange, though." I had made the hilt hollow solely to make it lighter. It was basically a steel pipe with a spearhead on top. That gave it more endurance than standard spears, but I had no idea if it was any sharper as a result.

"So, we ready?" Everyone nodded in response. I unholstered the New Model Army and loaded it with bullets from my waist pouch. Specifically, the bullets imbued with a small explosion spell.

I aimed at the jizo statue in front of me. It seemed like an action that would wind up getting me cursed, but there was no other option. Once I pulled the trigger, the jizo shattered into countless pieces.

With the barrier destroyed, I took out my smartphone, turned on the map app, and ran a search for the oni mask soldiers.

*Yup, it works. I can use my phone's functions again.*

I locked on all the oni mask soldiers, planning to take them all out.

"H-Hey, what's that?!" Yamagata and the other two looked up at the night sky with wide eyes. They were staring at the small [**Multiple**] magic circles. Leen was looking over at them as well.

"You're doing that again?"

"It's a good idea to get rid of all those who could get in our way, right? Things would get pretty bad if we teleported there and instantly got surrounded." I raised my hand to the sky, focused my magic, and activated all of the [**Multiple**] magic circles.

**"Strike true, Light! Sparkling Holy Lance: [Shining Javelin]!"** Light rained from the skies for the second time in recent history. The dead of night made it a beautiful sight, much like a meteor shower.

*But man, I wasn't among the enemy forces last time, so I had no idea it was so loud and made the ground shake this much…*

Spears of light fell all over the stronghold, destroying the oni mask soldiers one by one. It didn't matter if they were outside or indoors, the spears reached their targets even if they had to pierce through roof tiles. *Crap… I didn't really think this through.*

Once the rain of light stopped, I could hear the normal soldiers start to shout that they were being attacked, so I locked on to all the 'enemy Takeda soldiers' and cast [**Paralyze**], making the area turn quiet.

"Okay, let's go."

"Hey… Did you really just do all that?!" Old man Baba looked around while blinking in disbelief. For a brief while, the other two's mouths were open wide due to the shock, but they soon spoke up.

"Dear me… This is unbelievable…"

"Okay now, don't you think you took care of Kansukay with this?" It was a possibility, considering that 'enemy Takeda soldiers' included him, as well. I didn't expect him to be harmed, though. Not only was [**Paralyze**] weak against anyone with talismans, but it didn't have much of an effect on anyone with high magical aptitude.

"I think Kansukay's just fine. It's not a problem, though. Just means we have to take him head-on. Let's go finish this." I opened a [Gate] to the central quarter, where Kansukay was.

Once I was through the portal of light, I saw a one-eyed, swarthy man standing in the large garden. He was surrounded by immobilized Takeda soldiers. The eyepatched man noticed our sudden appearance and looked right at us, his shadow dancing due to the two bonfires next to him.

"I see. So the Elite Four are responsible for this, then? You've truly surprised me. How did you accomplish this?"

"You don't need to know that. Now shut up and die!" Yamagata brandished his greatsword and charged at Kansukay. *Whoa, damn! Now there's someone who's quick to act! But I guess his appearance isn't exactly hiding that.* Yamagata Massakage — the captain of Takeda's shock troops — swung his blade straight toward Kansukay's neck. However, it was blocked by the katana of an armored samurai who jumped out from the side.

"Wha—?!" He was clad in red armor and a helmet with a lion decoration. The samurai's white hair danced around as he deflected Yamagata's greatsword.

A red oni mask was covering his face. He was almost two meters tall and had muscles so large that it looked like they were going to burst. *Wait… it can't be…*

"M-Milord…?" The hoarse voice that somehow escaped old man Baba's lips confirmed my assumption about the armored samurai.

That was Takeda Schingen. He who was once the lord of Takeda. Now reduced to a mere puppet under Kansukay's complete control.

"Kansukay, you filth! You'd dare to use Lord Schingen as a shield?!"

"A shield? I would never. Lord Schingen merely protected me. That's all. Though, I do regret pushing him into a situation that made it necessary. I shall call for a replacement." Magic gathered around Kansukay, forming a large circle in the middle of the garden. *That circle's element is... Dark! He's summoning something!* **"Come forth, Dark. I seek the service of bones: [Skeleton Warrior]!"** A skeleton crawled out of the magic circle. It was wielding a curved sword in its right hand and a round shield in its left. *Man, this Kansukay guy sure seems to have a thing for undead-related powers.*

"Blade Mode." I took out Brunhild and instantly transformed it into a longsword. The skeleton charged at me, so I swung horizontally and split it in half.

But the skeleton slowly began moving and regenerated, seemingly shrugging off my lethal blow. Its split spine shifted back in place and it got up, prepared to charge me again. *What the heck?!*

**"Come forth, O Light! Shining Duet: [Light Arrow]!"** I heard Leen casting a spell, and a moment later, an arrow of light pierced through the skeleton in front of me. The bones shattered into fragments, never to regenerate again. *Huh? Why'd that work?*

"Surely you know that undead are weak to Light magic, right? Pointless slashing gets you nowhere, dummy." *Oh, right.* I returned Brunhild to gun mode and reloaded it. I elected to use Light magic bullets.

I aimed at the skull of another skeleton coming toward me and pulled the trigger. The gunshot was accompanied by a burst of light that splinted the bones, preventing it from rising again.

I looked to the side and saw Tsubaki, old man Baba, and Naito valiantly fighting the living bones, whose regeneration made the struggle look fruitless.

"This is annoying. I'll just end it all at once." Leen released her magic, causing a magic circle to appear below her feet. It began to widen until it was large enough to cover the whole garden.

**"Come forth, O Light! Shining Exile: [Banish]!"** Right after she spoke her spell, all the skeletons in the garden burst into particles of light and vanished. *What the hell was that? That was awesome!* Guess I shouldn't have expected any less from the clan matriarch of the magically-adept fairies.

"Hmph… Light-element purification magic. Not bad at all. However…" The red armored samurai stood before Kansukay, ready to protect him. He aimed his katana at Yamagata, blocking his path and preventing him from moving forward.

"Milord! Please move aside!"

"Schingen-sama! Blast it all, that slimy wretch!"

"Look at how he treads over our feelings… What scum!"

"Heheheh, it's useless. Our dear lord protects me. I know full well that you are unable to cross swords with the leader you are so grateful to. That means you cannot lay a hand on m—" Before Kansukay could finish his sentence, Schingen's mask suddenly shattered. Things were dragging on a bit, so I shot it with my gun.

The armored samurai dropped to the ground face-down. The puppeteer no longer had any hold over it. *Cool. Destroying the mask really did stop him.* With the deed done, I spun Brunhild in my hand.

"Wh-Wha—?!" With a surprised expression on his face, Kansukay looked between Schingen's still body and me.

"Squirt, you…"

"Hey, I didn't even know him."

"That's true… Still, I would appreciate it if you considered our feelings, too…" Old man Baba and Naito both looked at me with shocked expressions, but I really didn't know how to react.

"H-Heheheh, impressive. But I still have this!" Kansukay took off the eyepatch over his left eye. There was a red, shining eye — no, a jewel — inside the socket. It shone in a mystifying, ghastly, ominous manner, as if beating like a heart. *Is that the jewel we were told about?*

"As long as I possess the 'Jewel of Immortality,' I cannot die! You can even behead me and still, I will instantly recover!"

"So you used the jewel's power to grant immortality to the oni mask soldiers?"

"Heheh, that I did! The negative side is that I can only give the simplest orders when the soldiers are too far away from me, but this Artifact more than makes up for it with the great magic power and immortality it provides!" Kansukay proudly answered Leen's question. It was becoming very clear that that thing was the cause of this whole troubling situation.

"Hoo-ahhh!!!" With a mighty war cry, Yamagata swung his greatsword down on Kansukay. The attack neatly cut off his arm, but it quickly turned into a black mist and vanished into nothingness. Moments later, Kansukay's shoulder grew a perfectly new arm.

"Wha—?!"

"I told you it won't work! I can regenerate no matter how many times you cut me! And it's all thanks to this jewel!"

**"[Apport]."** I cast a spell, and a small round object appeared in my hand.

*Well, he just said he wouldn't regenerate without the jewel, right?* I threw the shining red jewel into the air and caught it, just in case Kansukay hadn't realized what just happened.

"N-No!" He hastily placed his hand against his left eye. Obviously, the jewel was no longer there. *Wait. It occurs to me that this thing was in his nasty old eye socket for who knows how long… Ew. Ew. Ew. This is gross!*

"Y-You bastard! When did you—?!"

"My my, talk about having sticky fingers. Is that another Null spell?"

"Yeah. [**Apport**] allows me to instantly bring small objects to me. Useful in situations like this." Leen took a look at the jewel in my hand, quickly took it between her fingers, and examined it with squinted eyes. Her brow furrowed as her glare turned intense. *That thing's pretty gross, honestly.*

"Hmph, this one's really bad. It has a curse that gathers the negative energy from the surroundings and makes the owner's heart impure. It was likely applied by some weird wizard. Either way, it's the reason this man lost his sanity. Though, considering that a clean heart gets in the way of controlling corpses, I can't help but call it practical."

"I'm impressed that you can tell that much just by looking at it."

"Don't underestimate the eyes of a fairy." She proudly puffed out her chest.

*Guess I shouldn't have expected any less from the clan matriarch of the fairies. I keep forgetting that she's kind of a big deal...*

"Artifacts are magic tools from ancient civilizations. They're all extremely precious, but this one has absorbed so much malice that it's now safe to call it a concentrated disaster. It's best to destroy it." Leen raised her right hand, still holding the jewel, and aimed at a nearby wall.

"What are you doing?! Stop that!"

"I won't." Leen maliciously smiled at the desperate Kansukay. *Man, she really likes doing things that people don't want...*

Leen threw the jewel with all she had, making it hit the wall and shatter into many pieces.

**"GHaahgHGHhh!!!"** With a blood-curdling scream, Kansukay fell to the ground. After a writhing for a while, he stopped moving and began gradually drying up into a twisted, mummified form.

Soon enough, he became dust, and the gentle wind blew him away into the night sky.

"Thank... you..." *Huh? Did I hear a voice just now... or was it my imagination?*

"What... What just happened?"

"This means that Yamamoto Kansukay already died. Interacting with the jewel probably absorbed his magic, willpower, and stamina, among other things." After Kansukay vanished and left nothing but his clothes behind, Yamagata asked a pretty good question. Luckily Leen was there to clarify. *So, with the jewel destroyed, the body was unable to sustain itself? That meant he was undead himself, huh?*

"Ah, Lord Schingen!" Just like Kansukay, the oni mask soldiers turned to dust and disappeared into the night sky. I could only hope that this would allow them to rest in peace.

The Elite Four and Tsubaki put their hands together and sent their prayers off for the dead. Maybe it was because I was Japanese, but I couldn't help joining them.

Three days had passed since the incident with Kansukay.

Things were reasonably hectic at first, but the land of Takeda quickly regained stability and found a new lord. Apparently, Kousaka — the one from the Elite Four who asked for our help — was hiding Lord Schingen's child from Kansukay.

The necromancer was fully aware of the boy's existence, but with Lord Schingen himself already being his puppet, he probably just didn't give much thought to the child. At least, that was how it seemed at first glance. There was no doubt that this chaos was caused by none other than Kansukay, but I couldn't help but question whether the sorcerer we fought in the garden was acting out the man's own will.

I could've been overthinking things, but a part of me believed that even after the Artifact robbed him of his sanity, Kansukay subconsciously tried to avoid hurting the child of his late lord.

Regardless, the son in question, Takeda Khatsuyohri, became the new feudal lord, and the Elite Four were once again the closest advisers to Takeda's head.

Just to be on the safe side, I told them to avoid picking fights with Oda. Then again, considering that my previous world and this one weren't *completely* in sync, my worry and the warning might've been unnecessary. But I decided that if a few years passed and I was suddenly informed that Takeda had been annihilated, I wouldn't be very pleased, to say the least.

With the war between Tokugawa and Takeda settled, we decided to make our way to our original destination, the Ruins of Nirya.

We were told they were at the edge of Shimazu's territory, toward the southernmost part of Eashen. Luckily, old man Baba visited the place when he was young, so all I had to do was have him share those memories with me.

In all honesty, holding hands and touching foreheads with a burly old man felt like a weird party game punishment or something.

"Father, Mother, Brother, Ayane. I am taking my leave, I am."

"Alright, take care of yourself."

"Touya-san, please look out for my daughter." As we were giving our goodbyes to Yae's folks in her house at Oedo, Nanae bowed her head to me. Not knowing how to react, I bowed back in the same manner. Jutaro and Ayane stood alongside Nanae, smiling at us all.

"We'll come visit you again when we have the free time. You're welcome to visit my place in Belfast, too."

"We look forward to it." I gave Jutaro a handshake and opened a [Gate] to the ruins.

After we walked through, still saying our goodbyes to Yae's family all the while, we were greeted by a beautiful sandy beach.

An endlessly wide sea gently caressed the white sand. I could see a rocky area and a small forest in the distance, but that was about it as far as scenic diversity went.

With a single look at the map, I found out that we were on a small desert island. Well, desert might've not been the right word, considering that the mainland was only a two-hundred meter swim away.

The emerald green sea dazzled us with the sparkling sunlight it reflected. I recalled reading something about white sand being white because a lot of it was coral and shells that had broken into tiny pieces.

"Wow, it's so beautiful…" Yumina walked across the white sand, her eyes fixed on the sea. Kohaku was right next to her, clearly having trouble walking, while Paula the autonomous bear was frolicking about as if it was nothing. *Seriously? What the hell is up with the* [**Program**] *on that thing?*

In contrast to the bear, its master was gracefully walking on the sand with a parasol in her hands. *Wait, where did you even get that?*

"It's been a while since we've seen the sea."

"You've got that right, Sis." The twins embraced the salty sea breeze and went on ahead, leaving footprints in the sand behind them.

Yae started after them, but before she could catch up, she stopped to remove her sandals and socks. *Probably full of sand, that'd annoy me too…*

"Ouch! Hot! Hothothot!" *Come on, Yae. With sun like this, what did you expect?* It wasn't even midday, and yet the sun, hanging high in the clear blue sky, was already blazing down upon us. All the heat from the light turned the sandy beach into a minor inferno.

Yae opted to avoid the heat by hopping on one leg and then the other, hastily making her way to the sea. It looked like a weird dance.

*Well, this place would definitely make a great resort, but where exactly are these ruins? Wait, didn't Jubei say something about it being at the bottom of the sea? Is that really the case? I better make sure…*

I ran a map search for 'ruins.' Instantly, I got one hit.

Jubei hadn't been lying, it really was at the sea floor. According to the map, it was about a hundred meters ahead, beneath the waves. I couldn't see anything at a glance. *Guess we're gonna have to dive.*

"Leen. Do you know any spells that allow people to survive underwater?"

"I only know magic that lets people walk *on* water. I recall hearing of a Null spell that allows the user to breathe underwater, but I wasn't interested, so I forgot its name."

*Dang it Leen, that's the most important part... Guess I have to dive in and confirm the existence of the ruins first. If I had a bathing suit, I'd already be changing into it, but this world doesn't even have those. Going in with just my underwear would be embarrassing, too...*

I walked right to where the sea met the sand, where Elze, Linze, Yae and Yumina were having fun in the shoreline waves. From the way they were splashing about, it was obvious that they were enjoying themselves.

"The cold water feels so good! Sucks that we didn't bring our swimsuits. I wanna go for a swim."

"...Now wait just a minute. Swimsuits exist?" Elze's words almost made me freeze in place. I'd always been under the impression that this world didn't have swimsuits.

"Hm? I-I think most clothing shops sell them. I even hear that there are different types of swimsuits that are sold depending on the region." Linze answered my question. *Oh, so swimsuits do exist...*

"Well, we're already on the beach, so we might as well make the most of it." When it came to clothing, there was no better place for us than Zanac's shop, so I opened up a **[Gate]** that connected us to Reflet.

It had been a while since we last saw Zanac, so our conversation dragged on a bit, right up until he began talking about how he had recently stocked up on swimsuits to keep up with demand for the warmer seasons. It was a case of perfect timing.

I questioned the existence of swimsuit demand here in Reflet-not-by-the-sea and was told that people often swam in the nearby rivers or the lake about half a day's walk away from town. I was also informed that some of the more affluent locals even had private pools.

Since the girls were obviously going to take forever to choose their swimsuits, I told them that I'd pick them up later. I made a quick detour back home. If we were going to have fun in the sun, I'd do my best to make sure nobody was left out.

"The sea, is it?"

"Wooow. That sounds wonderful!"

"Miss Cecile, wot's the 'sea'?" My three maids gave their unique reactions to my suggestion. They weren't against the idea, so I opened another [Gate] and basically shoved Lapis, Cecile, and Renne straight through to Zanac's shop.

I then went to the kitchen and did the same to Crea. Her husband, Julio the gardener, was soon to follow suit.

Leaving the home completely unguarded was a bad idea, though, so Tom and Huck couldn't come with us. I made a mental note to make it up to them somehow later on.

Laim said he wouldn't go swimming, so I took him with me straight to Duke Ortlinde's house. After all, that was the house of someone who'd get really mad if I neglected to invite them.

"The seas of Eashen, huh? Sounds great! Let's go!"

"Father! He invited *me*, not you!" *Is this country seriously that lacking in important business? Why is a duke of all people so eager to go to the sea?* The duke and his daughter were in high spirits. Ellen, Ortlinde's wife, watched them with a wide smile on her face.

I was about to open a **[Gate]** to move the duke's family and their butler, Leim, to Zanac's shop, but then Duke Ortlinde said something absurd.

"Why not invite my brother!"

"Hohoh, Eashen's seas, you say? How considerate of my little brother to invite us."

"Ooh… it's been a while since I've enjoyed the salty sea breeze."

"…Don't you have government affairs to take care of?" As His Majesty and Queen Yuel got themselves excited about the prospect of going to the seaside, I cast a rainy cloud over their parade with my question.

"I have absolutely no plans for this afternoon. I was actually thinking of inviting Al for a game of shogi. It's been a while since our last game, you know? So there are no problems in that regard! I'm totally free! Ahahaha!" I couldn't tell if that was good timing or an ill omen. Either way, their regalia stood out like a sore thumb, so I had them change into something simpler. I was fairly sure that the sight of His Majesty's magnificent crown would make Zanac pass out and drop to the ground.

Then I went to General Leon to ask for escorts to make sure the king and his family would be fine. He didn't hesitate to say that he himself would take the role. *Wait, are you for real? You're the general! You have duties!*

"Heh! There'd be something terribly wrong if I didn't come with the good old king on his holiday! I'll have some fun, too!" Boisterous and intense as ever, Leon pounded on my back and further splintered my fragile spine. *Damn, that hurts!* I tried inviting

Charlotte, too. She was receptive, but then promptly shut me down when she learned Leen would be there. The trauma must've run deep.

Once the king and his wife came out in their simplistic, but still expensive clothing, I opened a **[Gate]** to Zanac's shop.

*Oh geez, there's a lot of people here now. Wait... I count two more than there should be. When did Micah and Aer get here...?*

"Hey, it's been a while. You doing well?"

"Elze invited us. We couldn't refuse a chance to go to the sea." *Ah, so it was Elze. Well, it's not really a big deal.* I began sending those who had already bought their swimsuits straight to the beach. It was getting annoying, so I just fixed the **[Gate]** and kept it open.

Once I was on the beach, I used **[Storage]** to retrieve some iron and linen, on which I used **[Modeling]** to create two simplistic dressing tents.

The girls got a big one, but us guys would do just fine with a smaller one. Elze quickly walked into the dressing tent and shooed me away. *You don't have to treat me like a dog, you know...*

I went on to make some parasols and beach chairs, followed by a sizable sunshade. Relaxation was paramount during a beach episode, after all. Things would get pretty sour if someone got heatstroke. Last, but not least, I used some rubber to make a few beach balls and swimming rings.

The more people got their swimsuits from Zanac, the more people came through to the beach. There was quite the crowd by the time everyone was done.

Myself, Elze, Linze, Yae, Yumina, Leen, Lapis, Cecile, Renne, Crea, Julio, Laim, Duke Ortlinde, Ellen, Sue, Leim, His Majesty the King, Queen Yuel, General Leon, Micah, and Aer. Not counting the two small creatures... We amounted to a grand total of twenty-one. Almost a whole third of us were royalty, too. Though, there were things to be said about men being outnumbered in a similar proportion.

*Alright, with all of us kitted out in our swimsuits... Laim and Leim not included, I guess it's time to close up the* [Gate]*... Wait... Crap, I forgot my own!*

I rushed back through and bought a simplistic one-size-fits-all pair of swimming trunks. They were black and weren't made of nylon or polyester, but the material wasn't too different from them. It was nicely elastic and even had water-repelling properties. I asked Zanac, and he told me that it was made from the threads of cocoons made by a waterside bug called the 'Aqua Butterfly.' Apparently, it was often used for fancy umbrellas.

I thanked Zanac, went back to the beach, and created a fixed [Gate] leading to the living room of my house back in Belfast. I didn't really want to bother making a toilet or anything, so that would work just as well.

*Now, for food... it's gotta be a beachside barbeque.* All I had to do was prepare an iron plate and charcoal fire. We had quite a lot of meat and vegetables in our pantry, after all. *Wait, what about drinks...? Ah, I can just magic up some icy containers and cool down some fruity water. Oh, what about... Wait... is it just me, or am I the only one doing any work around here? No, it's clear as day! Nobody's even trying to help me out here! Damn you all! I want to have fun, too! Hm...? Wait, why'd we even come to the beach in the first place?*

I changed into my swimming trunks, walked out on to the beach, and began doing warm-up exercises. Well, I actually had no idea what kind of exercises I should be doing to prepare for a swim, so I just went with the radio calisthenics I was used to. As I faced the ocean and did my one-two-threes, I suddenly heard someone call out to me.

"What kind of dance is that?" I turned around to see Elze, who was already in her swimsuit. Linze was standing right behind her.

The designs of their bikinis were exactly the same, plain with white borders. However, Elze's was red, while Linze's was blue. The bottom part was a low-riser that had to be tied on the side.

Linze was also wearing a long, pastel blue parka. I figured she was shy about her attire. It went without saying that they had beautiful bodies, and honestly, I had trouble figuring out where to fix my gaze. I was quickly able to confirm that the little sister was the one with the bigger breasts, though.

"It's not a dance. I'm doing warm-up exercises. Don't want to just jump in and get an instant foot cramp, you know?"

"Oh, alright then. Is that how it works? Well, I'll just go ahead and believe it, I guess." *It's a fact, damn it! I don't need you to believe me.* I glared at Elze as she lightly turned her wrists and ankles, stretched her leg tendons a bit, spun her waist, and ran straight into the sea.

"Oh, I see that Elze-dono is already in the water, she is. I shall join her, then." Yae was already at my side, smiling at what she was seeing. I hadn't even noticed her approach. She was wearing a light purple bikini that had to be tied at the sides, and a halterneck. A part of me expected her to wear a sarashi and a red bikini, but I decided to never speak a word about that. After all, that would be her usual underwear, and this was a situation for swimwear.

*Oh, now's my chance to get a better look at them... They're huge. Whoa... she always binds them up with a sarashi, so the difference between this and her normal appearance is really throwing me off.*

Yae completely ignored my dumbfounded stare and ran into the water.

"You're not gonna swim, Linze?"

"Ah, I-I'm not very good at swimming, so I'll just rest in the shade…" Linze walked into a nearby area devoid of sunlight. Linze didn't seem like an especially healthy type of girl. I could only hope that she didn't get sunstroke or something.

"Touya!"

"Oi bruv!" Right on cue, the littler ladies stampeded toward me.

Both of them were in one piece swimsuits. Sue's was yellow and had frills all over the chest area, while Renne's was red with white dots all over and frills around the waist.

They both looked simply adorable. There was no risk of me getting nervous or shy around those two. Sue was in a swimming ring, while Renne was holding a beach ball.

"Make sure not to go too far into the sea. Not like it's deep around here, but still, you should stick close to the others."

"I know. We'll be just fine. Let us go, Renne! Onward!"

"Gotcha, Sis!" Sue took Renne's hand and led her to the water. *"Sis," huh? Well, I'm just glad they're getting along so well.* With Renne being younger, I got the impression that Sue was enjoying being able to play "big sister" with her.

"They get along soo nicelyyy."

"Whoa?!" Cecile's voice startled me into backing away. I'd have preferred it if she didn't approach people without giving away even a hint of her presence. Then again, it really showed what her real vocation was. Cecile was wearing an emerald green bikini with a pareo of the same color wrapped around her waist. It was a standard swimsuit, with no suggestive properties to speak of.

That being said… her breasts were even larger than Yae's, and I couldn't help but give them an occasional glance. *I always thought they were big, but that chest might even pass "large" territory and go deep into "huge." Guess this is the true power of maturity that I've heard so much about. She's fully equipped…*

"Lady Sueee, Renneeee! Let me join youuu!" Cecile began running. I keenly observed her movements.

*…Boing… Boing… Boing… Boing…* Say it once, say it twice — it was quite a sight.

"I wonder if large ones really *do* float…"

"Large what?"

"Hyahh?!" Lapis was standing behind me with a puzzled expression on her face. *Again?! Quit hiding your presence, damn it!* "What's supposed to float?"

"Huh?! W-Well, the swimming ring, of course! I was wondering if it'll float okay!"

"…It seems to be floating just fine, sir."

"Sure is!" Lapis, who was watching Sue and the others, was clad in a navy blue swimsuit that looked like a combo of a tube top and shorts. For some reason, she was holding a silver tray.

"What's that?"

"Well, there's work to be done. I was just bringing some drinks to the Ladies and the others." Lapis looked away and I followed her gaze to see the queen and the duke's wife reclining on beach chairs beneath a parasol. The table between them had a pair of tropical drinks placed on it, seemingly brought there by Lapis.

"Lapis… you're free to relax, you know?"

"Ah, don't worry about me. I'm having lots of fun! Cecile and I are switching work shifts now and then." With a broad smile on her face, Lapis walked through the [**Gate**] leading to our house. She was truly an exemplary maid. I shouldn't have expected anything less from a member of the Maid's Guild.

*Huh...?* I heard a loud noise, turned to its source, and saw His Majesty the King divebombing into the water. *Th-That doesn't look safe... Oh, he popped out. Guess that spot must be pretty deep.* Duke Ortlinde and General Leon were soon to follow after him. *Are they... Are they racing? What the hell are they doing now...? These three grown men are acting like little kids.*

"Touya." I was staring at the king and his friends, completely weirded out by their frolicking antics, when Yumina called out to me. The cutesy white bikini with frills on the chest piece and waist looked really good on her. She spun around and looked straight at me.

"Well? Any thoughts?"

"It looks great on you. You're adorable."

"Eheheh. Thank you very much…" *Huh, that praise came pretty naturally... Is it because I still view her as a child? Guess it must be that. Actually, now that I think about it, I'm not getting flustered or shy looking at her body. Guess she just can't capture my heart as she is now.*

"Touya, shall we go swim together?" Yumina hugged my arm. *Uhh... You're pressing your chest against me...* I couldn't tell if she was doing it on purpose or not. *I didn't realize it before... but she's showing clear signs of development...*

*It's soft... Oh no, my face is gonna turn red, ack...! Wait, I* **am** *getting flustered! "Can't capture my heart," my ass! SHE'S CAPTURING IT RIGHT NOW! HELP!*

"I-I have to investigate the ruins, you know. I'll come with you when I'm done with that." I slipped out of Yumina's grasp and made a quick promise. She seemed slightly dissatisfied, but didn't take too long to agree.

"Make sure to come play with me when you're done, okay?" Yumina ran off after Sue with a smile on her face.

*Man, that was close... My mental defenses were crumbling just there. Well, maybe it wasn't so bad... Or was it, actually? Yumina is cute, after all. There's no real disputing that... If I was forced to say whether I liked or disliked her, of course I would choose the former. But I don't know if I can look at her romantically or anything... Alright, what about this... Yumina finds a guy she loves... and she's just told me she's gonna marry him. Wait. No, why would you think about that?! That sucks! I just made myself mad by thinking about something stupid! Ugh... what the hell... Was that jealousy just now? I'm... not really sure. No, no. It can't be that. Yumina is as dear to me as a little sister, so my fatherly instincts simply don't like the idea of sending her off with some random guy... right? Right. Surely. Definitely... Probably. I think.*

"Why the pensive expression?"

"Huh...?" I turned around to see Leen, clad in a black, adult-like bikini with white laces, holding a black parasol.

If she was so averse to the idea of bathing in the sunlight, she could've chosen *not* to wear a bikini, but calling her out on that seemed like it'd be some kind of inexplicable loss in the grand scheme of things. Also, there were things to be said about a person wearing such a bold, side-tie, low-rise swimsuit while having such a small build.

I wasn't going to say anything until I saw the autonomous bear doing warm-up exercises while wearing a red and black border swimsuit straight from the early 20th century.

"Wait. Paula, you're actually gonna swim?" She pounded her chest as if to say "Of course I'm gonna swim!" I gave Leen a questioning glance, and the fairy chuckled in response.

"I didn't give her my [**Protection**] for nothing. She's completely waterproof."

*Man,* [**Protection**] *seems like a great spell. I'll have to cast it on my smartphone. On the subject of my smartphone, I left it in the changing tent. I wonder if Kohaku's still resting there.*

"Well, I figure it's time to go for a swim." I began making my way to the sea, and Paula wasn't far behind me. *Is she really gonna be okay?*

Paula made it to the shoreline, prepared herself for an amazing run into the water... and was promptly smacked in the face by a wave. She rolled back to the beach. Not one to give up, Paula charged back toward the seas. And, like clockwork, a wave hit her and sent her rolling back to the beach. I had no doubts she'd be trapped in this loop all day.

I shifted my attention away from her and ventured into the sea. I reached the point where my feet were unable to touch the ground and shifted to a breast stroke.

*Should be around here...* I took a deep breath and dove downward.

The water was crystal clear, so I could see everything below and around me without much trouble. There it was, the ruins I'd been seeking. Various large slabs were laid out in a stone circle, in the center of which was a small building that resembled a temple. I dove further down and looked inside the entrance to see a staircase leading down.

It was dark in there, so I couldn't be sure, but I had a feeling it went really far down. At that point, I really needed to catch my breath, so I swam back up to the surface.

I wasted no time. After getting a fresh intake of oxygen, I dove down once more. I instantly went straight for the stone stairs underneath, but again I was thwarted by my puny human lungs.

*There's just no way I can do it like this. I can only hold my breath for about a minute.*

I desperately wanted to know what was at the bottom of those stairs. I wanted to find out, but there was a limit to what I was capable of. I didn't accomplish much, but that was the best I could do. I had no choice but to return to the shore.

Once I got back, I saw Paula facing the waves and wiping the imaginary "blood" from her mouth, as if to say "You're... pretty good." *She's still trying?*

I told Leen of what I saw and sat myself down on the beach.

"So it's at the very bottom of the sea, is it...? What should we do now, then...? Perhaps I should try calling Marion?"

"Marion?"

"The clan matriarch of the Marines from Mismede. An old friend of mine. She'd have no problem doing things underwater... but it just so happens that she's quite the recluse." Leen folded her arms and began thinking.

I tried suggesting inviting any others of that species, but according to Leen the "recluse" part referred to a policy shared by all Marines who lived in Mismede. In short, they did everything they could to not meddle in the affairs of surface-dwellers, so getting *any* of them to come wasn't an option.

"It's surprising that a race like that agreed to take part in the founding of Mismede."

"That's the result of my negotiation ability. She's not a bad girl, and if you know someone for a hundred years, you tend to become able to tell what they're thinking." *A hundred years...? Geez, the scale of what Leen talks about is always too great for me to process.*

"Well, let's leave it at that for today. Go and have some fun now. If I keep you to myself for too long, the others will come to bear a grudge on me, I'm sure." With those words as her last, Leen went to Paula. *The others?* Suddenly, my sense of smell was overwhelmed by the attractive scent of cooked meat. I stood up and looked to where the wind was blowing from. There, I saw Micah and Crea, both clad in aprons. They were standing and making merry before an iron cooking plate. Micah was wearing an orange bikini, while Crea's was striped with black and white. With them both being cooks, I wasn't surprised that they got along.

Not far from them, I saw Aer, who was wearing a flower-patterned one piece swimsuit, getting Linze to cool down a metallic container. *Oh, guess they're making ice cream. Looks like that'll be our dessert, then.*

I then noticed Julio bringing ingredients through the [Gate] leading to our home. Apparently, the straw hat I got him became a part of his look. I hadn't seen him take it off yet.

I decided to help out, but as I walked over there I noticed something that needed my attention.

"...What are you doing?" Two butlers, ignoring the deadly heat and still wearing their usual pitch black suit and white glove combo, were looking at something through pairs of opera glasses.

"To see if she is safe, I am observing Miss Sue."

"For the same reason, I am observing the princess."

*...These brothers seem a tiny bit overprotective. Wait, Leim's master is the duke and Laim is* **my** *butler. What about ensuring* **my** *safety?*

Well, I didn't see the point of saying that, so I just left them to their business and made my way over to the food. I had worked up quite the appetite.

"Alright, now..." A day had passed since our beach party, and I had resolved to actually make some progress toward getting a look inside the underwater ruins. However, I had absolutely no idea where to begin.

"If only I had a spell that would let me repel water or breathe under it..."

"How about we build a tall wall around the ruins and drain all the water...?" *And just how do you expect me to do that, Elze?*

"Um... I-I just thought of something..." Linze timidly raised her hand. *Well now, that's a rare sight.* Linze wasn't one to volunteer her opinion often. Because of that, I assumed she must have had some kind of revolutionary idea.

"So, what is it? If you have a good idea, let's hear it."

"I-I don't know if you can call it an idea, but... wh-why don't you just send your vision there with **[Long Sense]**...?"

"......Oh." *Right. There's nothing stopping me from doing that. Why didn't I think of that? Am I retarded?* I wordlessly gave Linze a thumbs-up and cast **[Long Sense]**.

I quickly cast my vision into the sea and got a look inside the ruins. *Hm... this is...*

"Well? See anything?"

"…It's too dark to see…"

"Get a hold of yourself, already!" Elze's verbal push made me hastily send a [**Light Sphere**] down there.

A part of me thought the orb of light would vanish once inside the sea, but that didn't happen. It was a silly worry, since it wasn't like it was a Fire spell or anything.

Soon enough, the surroundings around my disembodied vision grew bright. I moved the light in sync with the vision, heading further down the stairs.

Eventually, I entered a large hall. In the center, there was a platform with a magic circle inscribed on it, surrounded by six pedestals. Each had a spellstone embedded in it. Red, blue, brown, green, yellow and purple — all the magic schools except Null were represented by a shining jewel.

Aside from that, there was nothing notable. No treasure chests, no inscriptions — nothing at all. *Was that really it?* I returned my vision and told Leen about what I saw. The clan matriarch of the fairies folded her arms, took a moment to think about something, and finally spoke up.

"That was probably a teleportation circle."

"A what now?"

"I think that when you activate the six elements around it, the magic circle will transport you elsewhere. It'll work in a similar fashion to your [**Gate**] spell, I believe."

*Hmm… A teleportation device for fast movement between locations, huh? I wonder if the sea level used to be lower in the past… Maybe people used that place as a normal means of transportation? Maybe the ruins are only abandoned because the sea level got higher?*

"I'd like to activate it… But that isn't exactly possible if we can't even get there. I guess we'll have to search for Null magic that allows you to breathe underwater and…"

"My master, if I might interject for a moment." Kohaku, who was nestled in Yumina's arms, suddenly spoke up and prevented Leen from continuing her train of thought.

"What's up, Kohaku?"

"I happen to know someone who can help you with your predicament."

We moved away from the beach and closer to the rocky area, where Leen conjured up a large magic circle.

"You are aware that summoning magic doesn't allow you to pick who you want to summon, yes?"

"Fret not, we shall mix master's magic power with my spirit power. If we do that, the one I desire to bring here will surely hear and respond to the call." Kohaku brushed away Leen's words. I hadn't the faintest idea that was an option. I figured it was just some kind of special-case workaround.

"But even so… to summon the Black Monarch of all things… I'll confess that I'm extremely surprised to discover that the tiger here is the White Monarch, but bringing forth another of the Monarchs should be absolutely impossible…"

"It is best if you stop logical thought when it comes to Touya-dono, it is." As Leen mumbled, Yae gently talked her down and left the magic circle.

"Summoning them should be possible, but I cannot predict what they will want for the contract to be complete. They are not too wild when it comes to temperament, but they can be quite, well… odd…"

"I keep hearing you use 'they' and 'them' when referring to the Black Monarch… He won't be alone?"

"How should I put this… the two of them make up the entity known as the Black Monarch. Well, you will understand once we summon them." *True enough. Better to get the summoning itself over with.*

I stood before the magic circle and focused my Dark magic upon it. A mist began gathering in the circle, becoming ever thicker with every passing second. Soon enough, Kohaku joined the magic channeling, charging the mist even more. Apparently, Kohaku's magic was called Spirit Power, but I wasn't one to care about such trivialities.

"O Beast who governs the winter, the waters, the north and the mountains. Heed my call. Heed my summons, present your form before me." The dense mist suddenly released a strong burst of magical energy. Or maybe it was Spirit Power, I couldn't tell. Just like the time I summoned Kohaku, I could feel the… whatever power overwhelm my surroundings.

Once the mist dispersed, a gigantic turtle appeared before me. It was about four meters in size. Or maybe it was a tortoise. They were both pretty similar. Just like any tortoise, it also had just four legs. However, it had characteristics which distanced it from normal tortoises and made it look closer to some kaiju from monster movies. More specifically, it reminded me of that one kaiju that could fly through the sky by launching jets from its shell. Though, the one before me didn't have that kaiju's large fangs, and its expression didn't seem nearly as menacing.

A black serpent was wrapped around the kaiju-tortoise-turtle thing. Just like the tortoise, it was quite large, too. It was larger than an anaconda. Its scales shone like black pearls and its golden eyes gleamed brightly. Those eyes were fixed on Kohaku, and myself.

"Oh myy... Sso it really iss the White Monarch. Haven't sseen you in forever. You doing okay, ssweetheart?"

"It's been quite a while, Black Monarch."

"Oh, come onnn, darling. Didn't I tell you to call me Blackie?"

*Man, this thing sure sounds carefree. But what the heck is up with this snake? Yeah, he sure is friendly... but maybe a little too friendly. His voice sounds kind of thick, too... Reminds me of a stereotypical drag queen...*

"And this young fella iss...?"

"Mochizuki Touya. My master."

"Your... master?" The tortoise suddenly glared at me. I felt as though I was being evaluated. Its appearance made me think it'd have the voice of a dignified old man, but boy was life full of surprises. The tortoise sounded more feminine than the snake. He did have a sharp harshness to his tone, though.

"To have such a human as your master... Oh, how the mighty have fallen, White Monarch."

"Say what you will. He will soon be your master, as well."

"Don't make me laugh!"

Kohaku calmly responded to the tortoise's provocation. Both the snake and the tortoise were now staring at me, the former with curiosity, the latter with anger. This situation was starting to feel a little troublesome.

"Very well, boy. Touya, was it? We shall test if you are worthy of contracting us."

"Fine by me. What do I have to do, though?"

"Face us in mortal combat. If you still stand and are in good health by sunset, we will recognize your power and permit you to make the contract. However, if you leave the magic circle, lose consciousness, or become unable to attack us, you can forget about it entirely." It didn't say anything about me winning if I defeated them. They probably believed that there was no way they could lose to me. Kohaku had mentioned that they excelled at defense, so that confidence was probably justified.

"I just have to stand around until sunset, right?"

"Yes. You can choose to run around, if you like. That is, if you believe you can keep running that long." The tortoise replied with a mocking chuckle. His arrogance was starting to piss me off by that point.

The magic circle was about twenty meters in diameter. It was definitely large enough to run around in. However, it was about to turn noon, meaning that I'd have to run around for a whole six to seven hours, and I knew that I'd reach my limit way before that.

Then again, that was probably the Black Monarch's plan. But it wasn't something I was going to let come to fruition.

"Alrighty. Let's get to it."

"T-Touya, are you sure you want to do this?" Yumina looked up at me, worry apparent in her tone and eyes. What a gentle girl she was. I calmed her down by patting her head. She had nothing to worry about, after all.

"Don't worry, Yumina. This'll all work out, trust me." With those words, I entered the magic circle. The turtle was still chortling to himself and, well, I didn't really care anymore.

"You're sssurprissingly calm."

"Indeed. I praise your courage, child. Let us begin!" As if to signal the start of the battle, the turtle let out a deafening roar. That was exemplary kaiju behavior if I ever saw any.

*Victory belongs to he who casts the first stone!*

"[Slip]."

"Hwuh?!" With a loud crash and a strong quake, the snake and the tortoise crashed to the ground. Considering how large they were, it probably hurt them pretty badly.

As I channeled the effects of my [Slip] spell, I reached for my waist pouch, took out a single bullet, and applied magic to it.

"[Enchant]: [Slip]." And so, I cast another spell, giving a certain function to the bullet.

**"Begin [Program]╱Starting Condition: The effects of [Slip] wear off╱Cast Spell: [Slip]╱Ending Condition: The original caster cancels the effect╱End [Program]."** *That should do it.*

"Guh!!!" The tortoise was trying to stand up, so I fired the bullet at the ground right under it.

"Gwaugh?!" It fell down once more, causing another quake. Again and again, the tortoise tried to stand up, only to spectacularly fall down and make the ground tremble.

"You... You're actually evil, did you know that?" Leen stared at me. The disgust in her eyes was palpable. I saw Kohaku, rolling on the ground and laughing loudly right next to her. The sight must have tickled the tiger's funny bone. Paula, too, was rolling with her paws on her stomach. *Just how much programming does that thing have?* Two hundred years' worth of code had resulted in something truly impressive.

"Once the effects of [Slip] wear off, another instance of the spell takes its place. When that one's gone, another is cast and, well... it's an infinite loop. Normally, the caster would run out of magic to sustain it in mere seconds."

*I'll have to thank Paula for this wonderful idea. I was inspired by seeing her get perpetually smacked by the waves yesterday. My magic regeneration is greater than the cost of sustaining the loop, so there are no problems in that regard.*

"Now, I just have to wait until sunset. Linze, you brought a packed lunch, right?"

"Ah, yes. I do have some, but…" Linze, clearly unsure about how to process the situation, looked at the Black Monarch. *Hey, I'm not breaking any rules or anything.*

"How should I put this… I feel quite bad for them…"

"I've seen Touya do things like this way too many times by now, and I don't think there's any point in saying it, but you should be more considerate of your opponents… Try to read the mood, I mean." *Wow, my methods are actually damaging my reputation… I* felt that was uncalled for, honestly. A fight was a fight, and if it there was a safe way to win without breaking the rules, it was only logical to take that option.

"Augh!" A thundering crash echoed out again. I unpacked my packed lunch and brought Crea's special sandwich to my lips. *Damn, this is a good sandwich. Can't really go wrong with ham and cheese.*

"Gyuh!" There was another crash. *The veggie salad's pretty good too. Man, what did she put in this dressing? Delicious!*

"Grruh!!!" And another crash.

"Hey, you guys. Could you stop that? I'm trying to eat over here."

"You're terrible!" Everyone in the vicinity felt like they had to yell that in unison at me. *What, really?*

"Don't you make light of me, impudent brat!!!" The black serpent finally roared something as he fell over for the umpteenth time. It was speaking in a completely different manner than before. *If you can talk normally, then what was with the drag queen mannerisms? Why would you do a character bit?!* It released a ball of water through its open mouth. However, since the snake fired as it rolled along the ground, the ball went to a completely different direction and hit the barrier around the magic circle.

*Huh, that actually looked dangerous.* Those outside the circle were completely safe, but it was clear that it could hurt me pretty badly if it landed a hit.

The tortoise saw an opportunity and, while airborne after a fall, opened its large mouth.

"Eat this!" It spewed water at me, compressed so hard it reminded me of a laser. Though, just like the snake's ball, it fired off into a random area.

The spell resembled Linze's [**Aqua Cutter**]. I knew that one could hurt me if it landed a hit, too.

[**Slip**] made the victim fall if they moved even a single millimeter, meaning that the very first fall would have them falling over and over forever. Aiming at and hitting me was difficult, but not completely impossible.

"Guess I've got no choice. I'll make you fall even more."

"Wh-What?!" Both of the beasts that made up the Black Monarch cried out in unison. I reached for my pouch, took out two bullets, enchanted them, and then loaded them into my gun. Instead of the ground, however, those two were meant for the snake and tortoise.

"**Nghuuaaooooh!**"

"**Ngyaaaaaaah!**" The two began to slip over even faster than before, ridding them of any opportunity for ranged attacks. They were falling so much that it seemed like they were inside an invisible washing machine.

"Wh-What did you do to them?!"

"Hm? I simply hit them with an acceleration spell."

"You're evil." Once again, everyone in the vicinity felt the need to tell me that. It was [**Accel**], one of my Null spells. It was meant to increase the movement speed of the caster, but as I just demonstrated, it wasn't impossible to grant it to someone else. Normally, it created a magic barrier around the affected person, but I made sure to keep it from activating. *What, why is everyone looking at me like that?* Even Kohaku had stopped laughing. Instead, the little tiger just stood there half-smiling awkwardly.

*I think I overdid it.*

"Ohh… Ghohhhh… It'ss sspinning… Th-The world is sspinning…"

"P-Please… No more… I don't wanna fall any more… I don't wanna slip anymore…" *Yep, I overdid it.* The black serpent's eyes were rolled backward and its head was lolling around, while the tortoise just wouldn't stop crying. It looked like they were laying eggs or something.

"Well… Sorry about that. Guess I went too far. Seriously, I regret it, I promise." I could feel everyone's cold stares from behind me, like daggers in my back. They accepted defeat and agreed to make a contract with me, so I dispelled the [**Slip**] loop. However, getting them to calm down took quite a while.

"Oh, that wass truly horrid… I can ssee why the White Monarch accepted you as masster." Even now, the snake's head was bobbing a little bit. The tortoise had already stopped crying and was now looking at me in a stoic manner. I patted its head and apologized once again. It closed its eyes and lowered itself before me.

"Mochizuki Touya. You are worthy of being our master. So please, form a contract with us." With those words, the tortoise and the serpent bowed their heads to me.

"Uhh… I have to name you, right?"

"Yess. Pleasse give uss ssome ssplendid namess, ssweetheart."

Kohaku suddenly chimed in on the matter at hand.

"Just 'Snake' and 'Tortoise' would be more than enough for these two."

"Shut that trap, punk! Ya pickin' a fight or ssomething?!" The tiger's words made the snake bare its fangs and spit verbal venom. Its true self was showing again.

I decided to keep quiet about the fact that I was actually just going to name them Snake and Tortoise. The snake's reaction made me realize it would've been a bad idea. I also assumed "Snakey" and "Tortoisey" wouldn't work, either.

*Just like how the White Monarch is Byakko, the Black Monarch is clearly Genbu, the Black Tortoise or Turtle that represents water…*

"Alrighty, it's decided. Kokuyou and Sango."

"Kokuyou?"

"Sango?"

When I saw those two, what came to mind was "black" and "water." So I named the snake Kokuyou, after obsidian, and the tortoise Sango, after precious coral. It also fit with the precious stone theme I'd given Kohaku. That tiger's name meant amber, after all.

"Do you like it?"

"I will gladly take the name Kokuyou."

"It is the same for myself. I will now respond to the name Sango. Use it as you see fit." I was glad they agreed. With their names set, the summoned beasts could now leave the magic circle. Sango slowly crawled through the barrier.

"Hey, wait just a moment, Black Monar— No, Sango and Kokuyou. We can stay in this world because of our master's magic.

However, your current forms would cause problems for him. You should change into something simpler."

"...Really?"

"Sso we should become ssmall, like the White Monar— like Kohaku, yess? Whatever you wish, Masster! Here!" Sango and Kokuyou instantly reduced their size. There was even a "pop" sound effect.

They had collectively become a thirty-odd centimeter long, black shelled land turtle with a normal-sized black snake wrapped around it. It was a… relatively normal appearance, until you noticed that they were floating in the air.

"You can float?"

"Only when we are this small. We cannot move especially fast, either." Sango began swimming through the air. True, he wasn't fast in any sense of the word. It seemed about the same as standard human walking speed. But man, seeing a turtle swim through the air was quite a surreal sight…

Still, at that size there'd be no issue bringing them along with me.

"Alright, Sango and Kokuyou. Let's get along." They came close to my shoulder and I patted them on their heads with my fingertips.

"I, Sango, will do my best to support you."

"Ssame here. I'll help you lotss, masster." That was good, because I had just the job for them.

"Sso we have to allow you to breathe underwater?"

"Yup. Can you?"

"Of coursse. None can come closse to uss when it comess to warding." The breathing part was settled, but there might've been other dangers. I decided that first, I would go there alone and activate all the spellstones. Since I had an affinity for all the elements, that wasn't a problem for me. Upon using the magic circle and seeing where it leads, I would open a [Gate] and let everyone join me.

"If something happens, use a [Gate] to return right away, okay?" As Elze and the others expressed their worry, I turned my back to them and walked into the water with Sango and Kokuyou still on my shoulder. *Whoa, my feet aren't getting wet.* There seemed to be a magic barrier about a centimeter away from my body. Sango and Kokuyou were already impressing me.

I entered the water with a splash. Soon enough, the water reached my neck, and a moment later, I was completely submerged.

I found myself facing no difficulties. I could breathe without a problem. Even water pressure had no effect on me.

"Just how strong is this barrier?"

"Well... When it comess to physsical attackss, it could even ward off a Dragon, but when magic iss involved, it dependss entirely on the opponent." Kokuyou answered with a slight sway of his head.

"We might be powerful, but there is nothing we can do against attacks that break through the barrier's limits, or spells that completely dispel the barrier." Sango continued the explanation. Basically, no matter how impressive, it wasn't the panacea to all defensive problems.

I continued walking along the seafloor. It occurred to me that the barrier seemed to be warding away the effects of buoyancy as well. I tried swimming upward to test that, and ended up floating a little bit, so I guess it wasn't *completely* gone.

I spent time pondering about the barrier until I finally arrived at the stone circle. I walked past that, making a beeline straight for the stairs in the middle of the ruins. With a magic light at my side, I illuminated the long way down.

Finally, I reached the large hall with the magic circle in the center. It looked the same in person as it had with [**Long Sense**]. It was surrounded with six spellstone pedestals.

I approached the red spellstone pedestal and filled its jewel with fire magic.

Moments later, the pedestal itself began to emit a reddish light. It was safe to assume that I'd activated it.

I continued to do the same with all the other spellstone pedestals. After making five lights come alive, I made my way to the final spellstone and filled it with water magic. Then, the entire magic circle began to shine.

"Guess this means I activated the teleportation circle." I hesitantly stepped on it… And nothing happened. *Huh? Why, though? The six pedestals are all shining and… oh…*

*Does it need Null magic after all?*

My [**Gate**] was a Null spell, after all. It was possible that the teleportation circle was based on a similar principle…

I stood in the center of the magic circle and focused my Null energy. The circle released a burst of light that was downright explosive! I teleported off in a flash.

I closed my eyes due to the sudden bright light, and after I slowly opened them, I realized I was in a garden. Blooming flowers, chirping songbirds flying around, there was even a small canal with water flowing through.

Just like in the underwater ruins, there was a magic circle beneath my feet. However, the six pedestals were nowhere to be seen. *Guess it was a one-way trip.*

"Masster… where are we?"

"No idea…" I stepped off the magic circle, looked around the garden, and noticed something approaching from the distance. *Is that… a girl?* Soon enough, I could see her clearly. So clearly, in fact, that I had no choice but look away from her. Silky, smooth, short, and jade-green hair. Porcelain-like skin and golden eyes. The girl had a thick air of mystery around her. When it came to age, she looked about as old as Elze and the others. That was fine by me.

She was wearing a sleeveless black jacket with a large, pinkish ribbon. She also wore white knee-high socks and black enamel shoes. That too, was fine by me.

Indeed, it was all fine. Except there was one thing that wasn't!

"A pleasure to meet you. I am Francesca, the terminal gynoid tasked with managing this Garden of Babylon." *Garden? Terminal?* Her words left me with some questions, but the biggest question of all was related to what I was looking at!

"Uhh, well…"

"Yes? What is it?"

"Why… Aren't you wearing anything… down there?" I knew it was bad to look, but I couldn't help throwing the occasional glance at her lower body, where I could see neither skirt nor trousers.

All she wore there was a small white piece of cloth. Her panties were completely exposed.

*Wh-Why?! Just where am I?! What is happening here…?!* I kinda liked it, though.

"I do not know how to answer your question. I believe you could call it a... duty?" The girl who introduced herself as Francesca tilted her head in a cute manner.

*Wait a sec, does she mean that wearing skirts or pants isn't allowed? Who's the manager around here? I have some compliments to give!*

*Wait, calm down... This situation is dangerous for your mental health.*

*I need to do something about this.*

"Uhh... Francesca, right?"

"That is correct. However, you should refer to me as Cesca." *Wouldn't Fran be the more logical nickname here? Ah, whatever.*

"Can you please put something on? I, uh... I'm having trouble deciding where to look."

"But I am wearing underwear, am I not?" *That's true, but so not the point here! Guh... Stay calm and keep it together, Touya. Just think of it as a swimsuit. It's a swimsuit, nothing more, and...*

I couldn't prevent myself from peeking at it again. *Nope! Those are panties, damn it! No doubt about it!*

"You just peeked, didn't you?"

"I'm sorry!" *Ah shit, she's on to me!*

"Well, if you insist, I will go ahead and put something on." Cesca pulled a black skirt adorned with white frills out of nowhere and began getting into it. *Why didn't you just wear that from the beginning?!*

"...Are you sure you do not wish to do something to me?"

"I'm sure. Just put it on already."

"I will not protest if you fondle me even a little."

"Enough of that! Hurry up and put it on!" I wanted to cry. I just needed to get her into the skirt so we could finally have a proper conversation, but the whole situation was mentally exhausting.

"So, I have several questions. Can you answer them?"

"Yes. I certainly could."

"What *is* this place?"

"This is the Hanging Garden of Babylon, high in the sky. Some call this place Nirai Kanai." *Hanging garden? The sky?* I looked around and it definitely was a garden, but it didn't seem any different from your standard botanical ones. I could see the sky through a glass dome above us. Cesca led me to the edge, where there was a wall of glass separating us from the outside.

Beyond it, I could see a sea of clouds. There was no doubt about it. The place actually was floating in the sky. It was well deserving of its name, a hanging garden.

"What's the purpose of this place? Why was it made?"

"The construction of this hanging garden was Doctor Babylon's hobby."

"Doctor Babylon…?"

"Doctor Regina Babylon. Our creator."

*Creator? What a weird thing to say. She's making it seem as though she was a product and… wait a sec.*

"My lord. This is not a human. I cannot feel the flow of its vitals."

"Wha—?!" Sango told me exactly what was on my mind. Both my understanding and my lack of comprehension of the situation crashed into each other at once.

"Dr. Babylon created me to be the management terminal of this garden. That was five thousand and ninety two years ago."

"Five th— Huh?!" *Leen told me she was six hundred and twelve, and I'm supposed to believe that this girl is almost four thousand five hundred years older than her?! Wait, I guess calling her a girl isn't right, is it? If she was created, then she's a robot...? Wait, is she an android? Or I guess a gynoid? I think she said something like that...*

"So, Cesca. You're a machine?"

"Not entirely, no. I have some magically-made organic parts and a magic reactor, so I am more of a combined magical-mechanical lifeform."

*Guess that makes her closer to a Golem or a homunculus, then... But man, she's so realistic. A normal girl from top to bottom...*

"...I am incapable of being impregnated, but I am well-equipped to partake in the relevant act, if you so desire."

"I didn't need to know that! H-Hey! Quit raising your skirt!" *Is she not programmed for standard shame?! Was Dr. Babylon a goddamn idiot?!*

"Worry not, my parts are fresh, clean, and like new."

"I didn't need to know *that,* either!" Cesca let go of her skirt, a look of disappointment clouding her face. Her mannerisms gave me a good window into the creator's mind. It was clear to me that Dr. Babylon was not right in the head.

"Thiss girl iss sso hard to undersstand." Kokuyou looked at Cesca, his head bobbing side to side. I couldn't agree more.

"That aside... I'm impressed that this place has been active for five thousand years. Is there a reason why either you or the garden didn't decay or break down?"

"The hanging garden in its entirety is strengthened by magic. Though five thousand years might seem like a lot to you, I was in sleep mode for most of it, standing by in case of an emergency. The hanging garden was largely automated as I slept."

*…Wait a sec. If she's active right now, doesn't that mean this place is in a state of emergency?* I asked the synthetic girl, and she gave a small nod.

"Emergency, indeed. We do not have a better word to describe it. You are our first guest, after all. What is your name, if I may ask?"

"Ah, I'm Touya. Mochizuki Touya."

"Very well, Administrator Touya. You have been recognized as compatible. I — Apparatus Number Twenty-Three, codename Francesca — have been assigned to serve you. Till death do us part."

"Excuse me?" *Compatible? No, wait… assigned?* Cesca pointed at the magic circle I used to teleport here and began explaining.

"No normal person can activate that magic circle. It is made to be unable to accept magic from multiple people. That means that it can only be activated by those with an affinity for all types of magic… Just like Doctor Babylon."

*So, the woman who made Cesca was just like me in that regard, huh? Wow, so someone else like that actually exists in this world… Well, it was a whole five thousand years ago, but still. So this place can only be accessed by people with the same potential as the old doc.*

"Dr. Babylon resolved to assign us to a compatible person who could make it past the teleportation circle. That was four thousand nine hundred and seven years ago."

"So when you say compatible, you mean people who have an affinity for all pools of magic?"

"No. That is not the case."

"Wait, I was wrong?!" She instantly shot my assumption down. *If that wasn't the condition, then what was…?*

"Administrator Touya, you were recognized as compatible because you told me to hide my exposed underwear when we first met."

"You can't be serious! How does *that* gauge compatibility?! That doesn't even make any sense!"

"Oh, but it is very important. If you had let your instincts dominate you and tried to have your way with me, I would have dropped you to the surface in but a moment. If you had chosen to ignore my attire and let me stay like that, you would have been deemed incompatible and I would have politely asked you to return to the surface." *For real...? Her exposed panties were that important?* I couldn't help but doubt her words.

"Dr. Babylon decided on this method to gauge whether a person is considerate and kind enough to be worthy of myself and the Hanging Garden of Babylon."

"I see... Dr. Babylon was some kind of freak, then."

"I will not disagree, Administrator."

*Seriously? The doc was definitely some kind of complete freak.* I couldn't stress it enough.

"Well, with that joke settled, I must reveal that it was actually left down to our own individual discretion. Personally, instead of a fake gentleman who is excessively kind and clearly used to women, I would rather settle for a 'secret degenerate' who throws glances at my underwear, but controls himself and pretends he doesn't care about it at all."

*Wait, so that's how it was decided?! I'm getting confused! And what did she mean by 'secret degenerate'?! That's super rude! The word 'settle' doesn't sit right with me, either.*

"At any rate, I am your property from here on out. I do hope we get along well, Master."

"Hhaahhh..." A sinking feeling came over me. I'd gotten into something troublesome. I could easily picture the twisted grin on Dr. Babylon's face.

I figured it was about time to summon the others. We all had a lot to talk about, after all. I explained the situation to Cesca and opened a [**Gate**] to the surface.

"A garden, is it...? This could be a relic left behind by the ancient civilization of Partheno." Leen was looking around, clearly overwhelmed by what she was seeing.

The ancient civilization of Partheno. It was a highly advanced culture responsible for creating various spells and magical implements, more specifically Artifacts.

This Hanging Garden of Babylon was a relic left behind by that civilization, and it was fair to call it an Artifact in itself. Going by that logic, Cesca might be considered an Artifact, too.

Everyone was walking around and exploring the place. Cesca told us that this hanging garden was the size of four Partheno Domes. That didn't mean anything to me as I had no idea what a Partheno Dome was. I had no doubt it was very big, though.

There were areas much like botanical gardens, fountains, stepping stones, flower beds, ponds — anyone even casually into gardening would go crazy over the place.

As I stood there admiring the flora, I could easily tell what was on everyone's minds. *Julio would love to see this.*

Leen, Cesca, and I were resting in one of the garden's corners, at a spot near a pool beneath something similar to a gazebo.

"So, you got what you wanted to find, Leen?"

"I'm actually unsure. I only hoped to discover some ancient magic, but we happened to find something far greater." She wasn't wrong. The whole of this hanging garden was one giant gathering of ancient magic. It had a garden that should never have survived five thousand years, but it somehow did. Then there were flowers that never withered, a barrier that made the whole of it invisible to outsiders, and so on... It was impossible for us to guess what kind of, and just how much, mysterious ancient magic was at work on this floating paradise.

Regina Babylon, the creator of this place, was a genius, no doubt about it. Though, it was kind of hard to ignore the fact that the good doctor was the type of person to force gynoids to walk around with exposed underwear.

"Cesca, is there anything more to this place besides the garden?"

"No. Nothing. Unlike the others, this Babylon facility is simply a wonderful personal garden floating through the sky. It has no treasure worth mentioning and no weapons to speak of. It is nothing more than a wonderful garden."

"Hey now, this place is a treasure in itself."

"That's very kind of you to say. However, you *are* aware that this Hanging Garden of Babylon is already yours, right, Master?" *Huh? What's she saying now?*

"The one that controls and manages this place is myself, yes? And I'm your property now, Master. That means my property is vicariously yours, understand?"

"...Are you serious?"

"Yes, I'm quite serious. You can consider it my dowry."

*Quite a big dowry, at that... Wait, what? I have no intention of marrying her! I've got enough on my plate with just one fiancee.*

"Hey, Cesca. You've now piqued my curiosity. You said that *unlike the others,* this place is just a personal garden. What did you mean by that?" Leen looked at Cesca with keen, perceptive eyes.

*Come to think of it, Cesca hasn't been referring to gynoids in singular terms, either... Her phrasing kind of suggests that there's more than just her.*

"Babylon is split into several floating sections. Besides this hanging garden, there's also the research laboratory, the hangar, the library, among several others, all of which are managed by my sisters. Babylon becomes complete when all of them are joined together."

*What...?*

"So, you're saying that the floating island of Babylon was created by your creator, Dr. Regina Babylon, some five thousand years ago. It then became separate and its parts are now floating all over the world, correct?"

"Indeed." Leen confirmed the facts with Cesca. The scale of it all was a tad too large for me to wrap my head around.

Everyone who had been out in the garden gathered in the gazebo and intently listened to what Cesca had to say.

"If something like that was floating around out there, wouldn't someone have noticed and made a huge fuss already?" Elze raised a fair point.

"Babylon is protected by a magic barrier that prevents outsiders from seeing it. Because of that, it is nearly impossible to view it from the surface."

*That seems about right... Dr. Babylon, the genius pervert of days long lost, must have used some kind of ancient magic to give Babylon the perfect stealth function. And the only way to discover it is by making it past the teleportation circle. A circle that would only work for those who had an affinity for all magic, just like the creator.*

"So, how many floating islands are there?"

"Besides my garden, there is the library, research laboratory, hangar, tower, rampart, workshop, alchemy lab, and storehouse. Nine in total, but I do not know if all of them still remain active."

*A whole nine?! Wait, considering they were all over the world, that number might actually be small. Plus, I'm pretty sure I remember hearing that the garden is the biggest of the individual pieces. Dr. Babylon was simply amazing... despite the perverted nature.*

"I'm quite interested in this library you mentioned. It seems like something that'd be full of knowledge about ancient cultures." Leen, sitting at my side, adopted a bold grin, but I wasn't sure if I could relate to her in that regard.

The library belonged to *that* Dr. Babylon. I would not have been surprised if it was actually a gigantic porn collection. It was way too suspicious.

I thought similar things about the storehouse, actually. I really did not want to go there and find a bunch of erotic goods.

"I-Is it possible to contact the other floating islands?" Linze asked a question, fear and apprehension laced into her words.

*Better work on that confidence, girl. You're still no good at interacting with new people. Well, I guess calling Cesca a person doesn't really count...*

Either way, Linze had a point. If the other places were controlled and managed by others like Cesca, then the most efficient way to complete Babylon was to get in contact with them.

"Sadly, the links between me and my sisters are now inactive. Our barrier is set to the highest level, preventing any and all magical communication attempts. Unless Master orders it, the defense level can't be lowered."

"What does 'link' mean...? And what exactly do you mean by 'Master,' here?" Yumina tilted her head to the side. She wasn't familiar with the word "link"? Guess Belfast hadn't progressed enough in scientific fields to let them know about technical terms.

"A 'link' is basically a connection between multiple things. And when I say Master, I mean 'my dearly beloved husband,' of course."

"Don't tell her lies like that. Master in this case is more along the lines of 'boss' or 'superior,' Yumina."

*Does she actually equate master with husband? How self-serving. Despite being an artificial girl — no matter how partial — she's too much of a jokester. I already know beyond a shadow of a doubt that this too is the fault of Dr. Regina Babylon. I didn't really think about this before, but Regina is a girl's name, isn't it? Well, she's definitely not the type of woman I'd like to have around…*

"And why exactly are you this girl's superior, hm?" Linze furrowed her eyebrows and pressed me for an explanation. *Wait, why am I being interrogated?*

"My dear administrator gazed upon my underwear, so I decided to dedicate my heart and body to him alone. That is why he is my master, the admin of my heart."

"Hey! You left out several key details just now!" The air around us turned sour almost immediately. Everyone in the vicinity with the exception of Leen, Kohaku, Sango, and Kokuyou was glaring at me with cold eyes.

Slowly, Linze folded her arms and stood in front of me. She didn't let me get up from my seat. Her eyes were emanating a light as cold as ice. *Wh-Who's this girl? What happened to the usual calm and docile Linze?*

"…Touya."

"Y-Yes?"

"On the ground, now." Linze was mad beyond words. Her voice suddenly carried an immense weight, probably because she was always so calm and quiet most of the time. I stood up from the chair and sat on the ground. I didn't want to risk making her any angrier.

"You've already seen all of us in our underwear, and yet you did it again with another girl? Do a girl's panties really mean *that* much to you?!"

"That was just an accident back then. I just happened to walk in and see it all, and…"

"So you did it on purpose this time, then?"

*Hey, there was just no way to defend myself from that exposure! She was the one showing them off to me! Why am I the one getting in trouble?!*

"So you weren't satisfied with seeing us in our swimsuits? I know you were looking at us a lot."

"Well… That was, uh…"

"I did my best to choose a bikini that paired well with my sister's, and that still wasn't enough? So you're the type to see a difference between swimwear and underwear, are you?" *Sh-She's being really scary!* Linze was looking away at nothing in particular, mumbling something quickly to herself. Even the other girls were a little confused. Leen piped up, a malicious grin spread across her face.

"Hey, shall I show you my panties too? Seems to be the fashionable thing nowadays."

"Sorry, but could you *please* shut up?!" Leen's grin only grew wider. She was clearly enjoying the unfolding scene. *No, but seriously… why am I being picked on? I didn't do anything wrong!*

"It looks like you don't know why they're mad at you." Leen shocked me stiff. It was as though she had read my mind. *Is she an esper?! Does she have some Null spell for that?! That'd be nice right about now! Gimme!*

"Just leave it at that. If you want to press him further, you should make your relationship with him clear. At the very least, you have to be on the same level as Princess Yumina here."

"...Yeah, okay." Leen's words made Linze nod and back off.

*I don't get it. They completely lost me.* I looked over to see Elze with a wry smile on her face. She was patting Linze softly on the shoulder. *I don't get it, but... it's over, right?*

"Only the master, Touya, can give the order that will lower the level of the barrier. At a lower level, communication should be possible. However, his administrative powers do not extend beyond this garden. Unless something causes the other facilities to lower their own barriers, we will be unable to make contact, is that correct?"

"Exactly." Leen and Cesca brought us back to the point of the situation.

I used my smartphone's map to search for 'Babylon,' but didn't get a single hit. Even the garden we were standing upon wasn't marked. I took that to mean the barriers prevented my [**Search**] magic.

"You've been floating about for so long. Surely you'd have encountered any of the other pieces at least once."

"Only twice. Once, three thousand and twenty eight years ago, and another nine hundred and eighty five years ago. The first time, it was the library, while the second encounter was with the storehouse."

*Good assumption, Yumina. But even so, that's a lot of years separating encounters. It's not like we can just sit around waiting for that to happen again...*

"So, to find the other Babylon pieces, we have no choice but to search for the teleportation circles, then." Leen heaved a long sigh. *Wait, we're actually doing it?* I couldn't help but feel a bit reluctant...

"Do you happen to know where the other teleportation circles are?"

"Negative. I do not even know the location of the one you used to get here. Where *is* the garden's teleportation circle, anyway?"

"Beneath the sea, just off the coast of southern Eashen."

"Eashen...? No such location exists in my database."

*That makes sense. Eashen probably wasn't around five thousand years ago.* Regardless, it was troubling that Cesca didn't know the location of the other teleportation circles. That would make things considerably difficult. Hell, the first teleportation circle was deep underwater. It wouldn't be unusual if the others hadn't survived the five thousand years they had to have been around for. That being said, finding them would not be an impossible task if they were all housed within ruins like the first one.

"Why was Babylon separated, anyway? Spreading it out all over the world like this just makes getting it back together seem almost impossible..."

"I am unaware of the reasons Dr. Babylon had for separating the facilities. I never asked, after all." I wondered if she had a particular reason for doing it. It could just as easily have been for a joke or something, after all.

*Geez, my faith in Dr. Babylon is going down the more I think about her. It probably isn't nice to assume that a person long gone was some sort of deviant...*

"So, Touya. What are you gonna do with her?"

"Not sure how to answer that..." Elze's question made me ponder. She'd been alone for five thousand years. That made her seem like quite a tragic character, but...

"What do *you* want to do, Cesca?"

"Well, I want to be with you, dear master. From dawn till dusk. From bathroom to the bedroom."

Those words made me feel uneasy. I was tempted to leave and pretend none of that day's events had happened. *Oh shit, Linze is mumbling something again!*

"Well… is it really okay for you to be separated from this garden? It can't sustain itself without your management, right?"

"No need to worry about that. I instantly know if something happens to the garden, and I have the ability to teleport here at will. The garden sustains itself just fine in auto-mode, so there are no problems in that regard."

*Damn it. My escape route is well and truly closed. Seems I've no choice but to take her, now.*

"With that in mind, I wish to register you as the garden's master. I am already yours, but I must make your ownership of the garden official, as well."

"Registration? What do I have to do?"

"Excuse me for a moment." Cesca walked over to me before I had a chance to get out of my chair. She placed her hands on my cheeks and, as if it wasn't a big deal, pushed her lips against mine.

"MmMpPh?!"

"AAAAAAHHHH!!!!" Four shrieks resounded around me. However, Cesca ignored them and continued to force her tongue into my mouth. *Whuh? He— Huh?! WHAT? What is she— Explain?!* Finally, she released my lips from the lock, which gave me a moment to process the fact that she had kissed me.

"Wh— Whuah?!" A strange sound escaped my mouth. But how else was I supposed to react? She had nonchalantly taken away my first kiss. She had stolen it from me, in fact.

The thief in question licked her lips as if tasting them and closed her eyes.

"Registration complete. I have consumed and recorded my master's genetic information. Ownership of the garden will now be transferred to Mochizuki Touya."

"Hey, what do you think you're doing?!" Yumina closed in on Cesca. With her small hands raised high, she was making her anger extremely clear.

"Wh-Who in their right mind just k-k-kisses someone like that?! Even I didn't get mine yet! I've yet to get mine, you know?!" *Did she actually just say the same thing twice?* Her face was beet red, and I couldn't even tell if she was mad or flustered. Whatever the case, for some reason, I found it rather adorable.

"I believe this to be the most effective way to retrieve genetic information. I cannot bear children, but the alternative retrieval method would've taken more time all the same."

"Ch-Children?!" Yumina's face grew even redder. I didn't know if it was just my imagination, but I swore that I could see some steam rising from her head. Suddenly, someone stood before me, blocking my view of the scene. I looked up to see Linze, glaring down at me with a stern expression. Her hands were on her hips.

Oh, things were sure looking grim for little old me. After all, I had enhanced senses that informed me of serious danger. I resigned myself to the fear and closed my eyes tight.

"Touya…"

"Y-Yes?!"

"I… love you."

*I'm sorry, WHAT? Her oh-so-sudden words made my eyes open wide, and when I looked up at her again, I saw that Linze's face was as red as Yumina's.*

She quickly closed her eyes, gathered her determination, and hastily pushed her lips against mine.

It was a kiss, no doubt about it, but unlike Cesca's, it was clumsy and forceful.

"Hgmgh?!"

"AAAAAHHHH!!!" A trio of shrieks echoed throughout the Hanging Garden of Babylon.

Some time had passed since Linze's confession. We were all flustered beyond words, so we took Cesca with us and returned home.

I quickly asked Laim to look after Cesca, hastily returned to my room, put my hands over my head, and dropped onto my bed. I was in a complete state of panic.

*What kind of situation did I get myself into? Linze is in love with me? "Love," as in... that kind of love? Oh man... Maybe I shouldn't overthink it. Linze is cute, no doubt about that. She's a graceful, calm girl. Always thinking of others. A bit shy, sure, but she more than makes up for it with how hard-working she is. She's definitely the kind of girl many people would be proud to call their girlfriend... But I'm still engaged to Yumina. Yumina's an adorable girl as well, and I can't help but admire the composure and reliability she has at such a young age. Then again, I find it pretty endearing when she acts her age, too. Am I just moved by the gap between her normal personality and her youthful actions? Hm? Wait, is it really a gap if her actions fit her age? Oh man, how the hell do I deal with this...?*

I buried my face into my pillow and sighed when I suddenly heard someone knock on my door.

"Touya, it's me, Yumina..."

"H-Huh?!" I opened my door to see Yumina, standing there in her casual clothing.

*This is super awkward... But why? I didn't do anything wrong. Is this how husbands feel when their wives find out that they're cheating?*

*Wait, we haven't even gotten married yet, so it clearly wasn't cheating or anything!* Yumina walked into the room and sat on the sofa in the middle. I nonchalantly sat in front of her, but I was unable to look her in the eye. I was unsure if what I was feeling was guilt.

Staaare…

Staaaare…

Staaaaare…

Staaaaaare…

*Guh… She's giving me the old heterochromic glare. Why is the air so heavy…?*

"Touya."

"Y-Yes?"

"I am quite mad, you know?"

*How am I supposed to react to that…? We happen to be engaged, so it should be obvious that you wouldn't enjoy seeing another girl profess her love to me.*

I did find it somewhat adorable how she furrowed her brow and pouted, but it did absolutely nothing to remove the weight from the situation.

"Even I didn't get a kiss yet, and now two girls got theirs before me?!"

"Wait, that's the problem here?!" *Well, that's all well and good, but I wasn't the one who kissed them in the first place! They kissed me! I don't care if that sounds like a cheap excuse, just understand that already!*

"You're not mad about Linze confessing her love to me?"

"Why would I be? Anyone with working eyes can see that Linze loves you, Touya."

*Well shit. Guess my eyes are on the fritz.* That made me feel a little disappointed in myself.

"This is a good opportunity, so let me tell you this. I don't care how many mistresses you have. It can be ten or even twenty, and I won't mind as long as you don't make them unhappy. That's just something natural for men, and I don't mind at all." *Seriously? I know that polygamy isn't uncommon in this world, but those kinds of numbers sound a little unreasonable. It's a little scary, actually!*

"However! HOWEVER! You can't be so careless as to get kissed when you still haven't even kissed your first wife! You have too many openings! Be more defensive! No, become impregnable!"

"Well, but—"

"No buts!"

"Okay…" A large part of me thought that she was mad about the wrong thing, but apparently, it was pretty damn important to her.

"So, you're saying that you wouldn't have any problems with this happening if I kissed you beforehand?"

"Well, I admit I would be a bit jealous, but I wouldn't be against it. So long as you properly treasure me, anyway."

*Is the person talking to me really twelve? Kind of feels like her views on things are a bit too objective, right? Does she really love me as much as she claims…?*

"…You just thought something rude, didn't you?"

"Uhhh…" *Why am I surrounded by such perceptive girls?* Yumina got up off the sofa, walked around the table with determination in her step, and sat right next to me.

"Touya. I am prepared to take you as my husband and live my whole life as your wife. That is because I love you. Because I love you just as much as, if not more than, Linze does. I don't want you to doubt that."

"…Sorry." My apology couldn't have been more sincere. Being so doubtful of her feelings was the height of discourtesy. I was at fault for not having been clear enough to her.

"…I really am sorry."

"…I'll forgive you if you hug and kiss me."

*Whoa! Talk about a difficulty spike! The situation's tough enough already, isn't it?! Then again, it really doesn't seem like she'll back down until she gets what she wants.* I fearfully reached for her shoulders and pulled her small frame closer. I pulled her into a tight embrace, the top of her head resting under my chin. The softness of her body and the feminine smell of her hair made my heart stir wildly.

*Alright. Okay. I have no choice but to admit how I felt about her.* Yumina slightly backed away from me, then slowly closed her eyes and tilted her face upward. *That's a clear sign that there's no going back now! Even I'm aware of that!* I steeled myself and kissed Yumina on her small, soft lips. It wasn't much more than a light, gentle touch.

I quickly reeled backward, pulling my face away from hers. She gave me a bright smile and tightly wrapped her arms around me.

"Eheheh. You kissed me! That makes me the first one *you* kissed, right?!"

"Er, well… Yeah. Guess that's true…" I was already kissed twice, but this was the first time I had done the kissing. *Wait, was that her goal all along?!* A part of me began to believe that everything that had just happened was all a part of her master plan, but the thought was kind of scary, so I chose not to dwell on it.

That aside, what would society think about a boy who's sixteen kissing a girl who's twelve…? I had no idea how it was in this world, but in the previous one, it would basically be a first year high schooler kissing a sixth year elementary schooler… And that seemed like a huge crime. Which was a little strange. I mean, considering that there was only a four year difference between us, it wasn't so bad…

"What do you think of Linze, Touya?"

"Well, I… I think she's cute and, honestly, I was kind of happy when she confessed her love to me. But I can't even decide how I feel about you, and now I have to think about Linze, as well, which is really nerve-racking. And yeah, I know that makes me sound pathetic."

"And if you had to say whether you liked or disliked her?"

"Well, obviously I like her. There's no doubt about that. She's dear to me."

Yumina smiled, still wrapped up in my arms. *What? What's with that sly smirk on her face…?*

"Did you hear that, Linze?"

"What?!" Yumina spoke toward one of the room's corners. I looked over there, and a moment later, Linze appeared out of nowhere, her cheeks red as beets. *Wait, what?!*

"We asked Leen to cast that spell on her. Without it, there's no way Linze would've come here."

*Wait, she was using* [**Invisibility**]*?! She was in the room the whole time? That means she heard everything I said and… Damn it, how embarrassing!*

"It's your fault, you know? You just shut yourself in your room without saying anything. Linze was actually crying because she thought you hated her. Elze was about to come over and punch your teeth in."

"Ahh… I'm thankful she didn't…"

*Geez, I was so overwhelmed by my own feelings that I didn't consider anyone else. I'm totally hopeless…*

"U-Uhm, I-I'm sorry about what I did. When I saw Cesca kiss you, I just didn't want to lose to her… And it happened before I realized it… I didn't even consider your feelings… I'm so sorry…" I closed in on Linze and took her hand in mine. She was trembling, tears running down her cheek.

"Ah…"

"As I'm sure you just heard, I don't hate you. I think you're cute and yeah, I do like you. I'm not sure how I should go about this, but I *do* know that I treasure you."

"Touya…" Linze faintly smiled. *Yep. A smile fits her face better than any tears could. And I'm the one who caused those tears. Elze could knock my teeth out and it'd be justified.*

"With both of your feelings settled… how about it? Will you take Linze as your second wife?"

"E-Excuse me?" Yumina nonchalantly said something unbelievable. *Another wife? Linze?* I looked at the girl and saw her fidgeting. Her face was still red as a tomato.

"It's fairly standard for royalty, nobility, and wealthy merchants to take second or third wives. The only issue is your dependability as a man. If you are able to properly care for us, no one will complain. I'm sure you're okay with that, right, Linze?"

"I-I want to be your w-wife, Touya."

*Seriously…? Well, that makes me happy, sure, but there's a lot of other aspects to consider here.*

"…D-Do you not want me?" Linze looked as if she was about to cry.

*Crap, I can't let that smile disappear. Making her sad again just isn't an option. Alright! Whatever! Come what may!*

"You're fine with being my second wife? Are you sure about that?"

"…I-I think I can get along with Yumina. If we can both find bliss while loving the same person, nothing would make me happier."

"…Alright, then. If you're really both fine with it… I'll accept the both of you." Suddenly, Linze smiled brightly and hugged me tight. With her usually being so docile, that action temporarily confused me. Yumina stood up and jumped at me, too. *Th-This is seriously embarrassing!*

"So, from now on, Linze is just like me — a fiancee!" Yumina looked really happy. Linze's face was still kind of red, but from the way she nodded, it was clear that she was happy, too.

It was already quite late, so I told them to go back to their rooms. They responded by asking me for a goodnight kiss. I didn't yet have the guts to kiss them on the lips, so I somehow got them to compromise, strange as it may sound, with a kiss on the forehead. Yumina was happy, while Linze was embarrassed.

After they left my room, I heaved a long sigh. *Way too many things happened today. I need to get my feelings in order.* As always, I lay down on my bed.

*So, how am I supposed to deal with this…? I have the money to take care of both of them, I have a proper house for them to live in. Do I even have any actual problems? Oh, right, I'll have to pay a visit to Linze's parents… All that matters now is my resolve. I have to be prepared to live the rest of my life with them. I have to think ahead about this… After all I… want them to be happy.*

I slowly fell asleep, with many thoughts gently bouncing through my mind.

**THUD!**

The door to my room crashed open, startling me awake. *Huh, who what where why?! Is it morning? The room's bright…* I looked around, half-asleep, to see a person standing by my bed. It was a girl. She loomed over me, the morning light shining down on her.

"We gotta talk. Now." It was the elder twin sister of the girl that had become my second fiancee just a day before. The morning light made the gauntlets on her hip shimmer slightly.

*Well, this isn't ominous. Could trouble avoid coming so early in the morning? Just once, please?*

Elze took me to the third training ground of the royal army. Elze and General Leon often used this place to spar, and Elze, despite being an outsider, was able to come and go here as she pleased. We had no trouble getting in thanks to that.

It was still early, so nobody was training. Besides the odd bird's chirps, the place was enveloped in absolute silence. Elze led me to the training grounds, and I saw that we weren't alone.

"Yae? What are you doing here?"

"…Touya-dono. I have been waiting for you, I have." Yae sat in the middle of the training field. Her blade was in front of her and her posture made it seem as though she had been meditating for some reason. Suddenly, she opened her eyes, grasped her blade, and stood up. She seemed slightly different to her usual self.

"You're taking Linze as your wife, right?"

"Ah… Yes, indeed, that happens to be the case…" I turned around to see Elze staring at me.

*There's that glare again… Just how many times and from how many girls have I received this glare in the last day or so? Then again, it's a matter concerning her little sister, so it's not surprising she's so serious.*

"So that makes you my brother-in-law, then?"

"Aha… Yes… I hope we get along well, indeed…" I hadn't really thought about it, but she was right. *Elze as a sister-in-law… Something is just plain off about that.*

"What do you think of Linze, then? Do you really like her?"

"…To be completely honest, I'm still unsure about that. I don't think I can say that I love her, but the same goes for Yumina, too. Still, I definitely like her as a person, and she's very important to me."

"And did she agree with that?"

"She did." Elze let out a sigh.

*Is she disappointed? Shocked? At a loss for words? I can't tell…* Elze briskly scratched her head and repeatedly, but lightly, kicked the ground with her toes, clearly irritated. *Whoa, she's scaring me!*

"That girl always had this side to her… Despite being such a scaredy-cat most of the time, she's always been the type to be bold where it counts. She's the complete opposite of me when it comes to that…"

"I am not too different in that regard, I am not. I am unable to become determined without a proper push…"

*What are they going on about now?* Elze equipped the gauntlets she had on her waist and smacked her fists together. The clang that echoed out was quite noisy. Yae, too, placed her sword through her sash and fixed its position.

"Touya… I want you to fight us."

"Huh?!"

"If you win, we won't say anything about your relationship with Linze. But if we win, you'll have to listen to our request." *Wait, what?! How did it come to this?! Am I being punished for something?!* Yae unsheathed her sword, seemingly ignoring my confusion.

"I borrowed this sword from Viscount Swordrick, I did. The edge of the blade is rounded off. It should not be able to kill or even cut you, but shattering your bones is well within the realm of possibility, it is." *That information does nothing to calm me down!*

"Touya, use [**Modeling**] to dull Brunhild's blade as well."

"Wait! Before I do anything, can you tell me why I have to fight you two in the first place?!"

"To be frank, Touya-dono. The both of us are the type of girls who need to do this, we are. It's a matter of confronting our feelings. If you wish to call it cowardly, so be it." I had no idea what she was talking about, but they clearly had no intention of backing down. *Alright, all I have to do is lose on purpose, and...*

"If you hold back, I'll never forgive you. I won't accept your relationship with Linze, either. I'll never allow my sister to be with a man who refuses to get serious when it matters."

*Crap. She warned me against doing exactly what I was planning... Guess Elze knows exactly how my superficial mind works.*

Reluctantly, I did as I was told and used [**Modeling**] to round off Brunhild's blade.

*Guess I have no other choice, I'll just cast [**Slip**] the moment the fight begins, and then...*

"No Null magic allowed. You can't call it a fight if we just drop to the ground the moment the battle starts. I won't use [**Boost**], either."

*How the hell did she know exactly what was on my mind?! Holy shit, women are scary!*

"Touya-dono can use elemental magic, as well as ranged and melee weaponry. We can only use melee weaponry, but there are two of us. That seems fair, does it not?"

*That means the only bullets I can use are the normal rubber ones. The impact from those things can really rattle your bones, though, so it's not like they're bad.*

"I still feel like I'm at a disadvantage, though…"

"I am fully aware that we are asking a lot of you, we are. However, we need an opportunity to take the next step." Once again, I had no idea what she was saying, so I just sighed and steeled myself. I figured I'd play their game as long as they needed me to.

"Are you ready?" I simply nodded, afraid to ask what I had to be ready for.

The next moment, Yae and Elze split up and closed in on me from two separate angles. *A pincer attack? Already?!*

"Blade Mode!" I extended Brunhild into the shape of a blunted longsword, then ran toward Yae. I could have easily parried her blade, but the same couldn't be said of Elze's fists.

After crossing swords with Yae, I used the momentum to slip past her. I turned around, took the New Model Army into my left hand, and fired all six bullets at her.

I was brimming with confidence, certain all six shots would find their mark on Yae's back, when Elze jumped into their path and held her left hand up high. The gauntlet she wore was shining an emerald green.

A moment later, the bullets scattered into several uncertain directions.

"As long as they aren't magic, ranged attacks don't work on me." *Crap, I forgot! Her emerald gauntlet was imbued with a wind-type barrier spell that deflected all physical ranged attacks!*

"Gun Mode! Reload!" I barraged them with all twelve bullets from both of my guns in a desperate attempt to distract them and buy some time.

But Elze didn't seem to care. She charged at me while holding up her left gauntlet.

"Blade Mode!" Elze's right fist closed in on me, but I was able to evade it. I quickly changed Brunhild into a longsword again and launched a horizontal slash at her. She evaded it, too, but it bought me some time to back away and fix my stance.

"You are a naive fool!" Yae came lunging at me from right behind Elze. I had no chance to distance myself. *Hold on a sec!*

*That'll definitely cut me, dulled blade or not!* I dodged to the side, preventing the tip of her blade from digging into my shoulder. Then, I quickly turned around and tripped her over with my leg, using her own momentum against her.

"Kuhh?!"

"Reload!" As Yae fell to the ground, I quickly aimed at her with the New Model Army.

However, before I could pull the trigger, Elze attacked me with a kick, leaving me with no other option than to back away.

**"Entwine thus, Ice! Frozen Curse: [Icebind]!"** My spell made the ground beneath their feet begin to freeze.

"Agh!" They deftly escaped and split up, coming at me from two angles again. The rimy binding didn't even have a chance to take hold.

*Crap! I'm at a clear disadvantage here! After all, it's not like I can do anything that could seriously hurt them or anything!*

"Whoa!" I evaded another straight punch from Elze. Yae was closing in on me, too. At that moment, I closed my eyes and cast a spell.

**"Shimmer forth, Light! Dazzling Brilliance: [Flash]!"**

"Kh?!" The sudden burst of bright light made Yae stop in her tracks. I used the opportunity to back away from them again. It was best for me to keep my distance in a battle with those two. I was at the greatest advantage at long-range.

Once she recovered from the blinding flash, Yae reached for her hip, took out her shortsword, and placed it in her free hand. *What...?* Yae lowered her posture and charged toward me. Right when I was about to fire a feint or two so I could make her back away, she actually threw the shortsword at me.

*Whoa?! Who the hell throws their weapon like that?! Doesn't the sword represent a samurai's soul?! Do shortswords not count or something?!* I barely dodged it by slightly moving my pelvis to the side. *Ugh! It grazed me!* Before she could fix her posture, I fired all twelve of my loaded bullets at her. *There's no way she can dodge at this distance!*

"Gah!!!" The strong rubber rounds made Yae fall to the ground. Despite that, she was still able to launch a horizontal slash at me. It was something I could easily evade, though.

But Elze was waiting for me, right at the spot I had jumped to. *Crap, she's too close! Her fists are way faster than my aim.* Elze went all out and attacked me with a right hook. *I don't have any other choice!* I bent my body and somehow dodged her fist, let go of my guns, and grabbed her right hand. I used my momentum to spin her around with her back facing toward me. Then, I put my right elbow into her armpit and raised her up.

"Wha—?!" I threw her to the ground, and she made a noise that sounded like a scream. I hadn't done a shoulder throw since school, but my body seemed to remember the motions.

"Gah…!" Apparently, my technique wasn't good enough to properly damage her. Elze quickly rose to her feet.

But by the time she was standing upright again, I had Brunhild trained on her. We were so close that she couldn't redirect the bullets even if she wanted to.

It has a classic hold-up.

"Reload. I win."

"…Why aren't you shooting?"

"Because if you accept defeat, I won't need to." Firing at someone dear to me didn't make me feel good. I made a mental note to apologize to Yae after the battle.

"You're stupidly kind. Do you really think you can protect Linze and Yumina with that mentality?"

"…That's just who I am."

"Heh, it sure is. Guess it's part of the reason why me and Yae fell in love with you."

"……What?" *What did she just… say? I, uh… What?* My brain functions froze up.

Just as I snapped out of my trance, I realized that Elze's right hand — the one clad in the red gauntlet — was emitting a light. *That gauntlet's ability was… increasing destructive power, wasn't it?! Alright, if she really doesn't want to fold, then I guess I can't go easy on her either.* I aimed at Elze and pulled on Brunhild's trigger. The battle was finished. Or so I thought.

"Wh—?!" I pulled the trigger a second time. It didn't fire. As it turned out, it wasn't even loaded. *What? Why? I'm pretty sure I reloaded… Oh…*

Yae's actions from earlier finally made sense to me. The shortsword she threw at me. She hadn't thrown it in order to harm me. When I dodged and it grazed me, the fastener on my waist pouch had been sliced open.

My bullets had scattered out of it as I moved, and they had all ran out. My reload was meaningless if there weren't any bullets within a radius of one meter… *I've been had.*

With lightning-fast speed, Elze stepped to the side and launched her fist into my chest.

"Gghuh?!" I tumbled to the ground, my consciousness fading.

"W-We want you to treat us the same as Yumina and Linze!"

"…Huh?" I came back to my senses and, since I had lost, readied myself for whatever their request was, but no amount of preparation could've been enough for what they hit me with.

"W-Well, surely you understand th-that we… We do… Ohh… Y-You should be the one to say it, Elze-dono!"

"H-Huh?! B-But I…! Ohh… W-Well, f-first up, uh… I-I-I also love you, Touya!"

"I-It is the same for me, i-it is!" They looked down, their faces flushed red.

*…What the hell? Weren't we just fighting a moment ago? Now I'm being confessed to? By two girls at once, even. What exactly is this?*

"Treat you like Yumina and Linze…? What do you mean?"

"W-We also want to become your… w-wives… we do."

"Y-Y-You have to agree to this, you know?! Y-You lost the fight, fair and square!" I pinched my cheek.

*Well, that hurt. Not dreaming, then. Guess I've got four incoming brides, huh? Wait! No no no no! Isn't that a bit too many?! But wait, Tokugawa Ienari had more than forty concubines and over fifty children… Compared to that, I guess that I… Wait! Comparing myself to him is insane! Seriously, that guy used to harvest the… you-know-whats… of fur seals, turn them into powder, and drink them for sexual vitality! He was even nicknamed the "Fur Seal General" because of that. I don't want to be grouped with a guy like him! Damn it, Touya, stop. You're going off on a stupid tangent.*

"Are you two… really okay with that?"

"I don't mind. Nothing's gonna change my feelings for you, and if I can be happy and others can be happy while loving the same person, then it's all good, isn't it?" I remembered that Linze had said something similar the day before. Those girls really were twins. Their thought patterns certainly matched up sometimes.

"I love them all about as much as I love you, Touya-dono. If we can all become your wives, then all is well, it is."

*Man, the girls of this world sure have a low desire to monopolize their man. Hmm... did they grow up to be like this because polygamy is the norm? Or wait, maybe these girls are just odd? Normally, this would be the perfect setting for a catfight... They don't really seem to be displaying much jealousy though, so it's kinda weird. Well, not that it didn't exist. There was some slight envy, as evidenced yesterday. Come to think of it, Linze might be the most jealous person among them.*

"S-So? What about you...?"

"Huh?"

"I-I'm asking about what you think of us!"

*Oh, that.* The recent barrage of romantic events made me feel a bit numb, and that wasn't a good thing.

I had to tell them exactly how I felt.

"If I was forced to say whether I like or dislike you, then sure, I *do* like you. You're both cute and have good personalities. But even so, I'm not sure if I can say that I love either of you. Just as I said before, the same goes for Yumina and Linze. I'm happy that you confessed your love to me, but I'm not sure if I can accept you on good conscience with my feelings being so vague."

"But you accepted Yumina-dono and Linze-dono, did you not?"

"I wasn't lying when I said that I liked them, and there's no doubt that they're important to me. They said they were fine with that, too."

*Honestly, the concept of marriage is still pretty unreal to me. Hell, we aren't even dating, so marriage shouldn't even be on our minds. My cousin skipped through the whole dating process and got married because he knocked up the girl, too. Now I have a closer glimpse into that poor bastard's situation.*

"So, that means that Yumina and Linze are fine with us too, right? Then it's all fine."

"But I have no idea what they'll say about this…"

"There is no need to worry about that, Touya-dono. The one who invited us to become your wives was Yumina-dono, it was."

*…Pardon me?*

"Right when the king gave you the mansion, Yumina secretly approached us. She asked us all how we felt about you, confirmed our feelings, and then suggested we all become your wives. We weren't so certain about it at the time, though. But, uhm… little by little… we began to think it'd be nice. Then when Linze lost her composure yesterday, I finally decided! I want to be by your side, Touya." Elze looked straight at me. There was no hesitation in her eyes. Her face was still a bit red, though.

"I began to think that it would be great if we could all live as a family, with you at the center, I did. In all honesty, I am still unused to Yumina-dono's leniency, but I have no doubt that I want to live by your side, I truly do."

*Yumina was the one who said she wouldn't mind if I had ten or twenty mistresses… Was that "leniency" just a display of her confidence as the first wife?*

"S-So?"

"…Alright, I understand how you both feel. I like you both, too. Elze, you're lively and cheerful, albeit a bit obstinate, but I find that pretty cute, too. Yae, you're diligent, dignified, and very considerate of your family. I'm also aware that you're gentle and good with children. You two would be excellent wives, I'm sure."

"Th-Then—" Before Elze could speak, I raised my hand to stop her.

"However, I need some time to think. I'll give you my answer in the evening. I've got some stuff to mull over first."

"…Alright."

"…I understand, I do." We headed back home. I went up to my room, while Elze and Yae went to have a talk with Yumina.

I sat on my bed, exhaled a long sigh, and assumed my thinking pose, flat on my back.

*What now? Well, the answer to that question is already obvious. I already accepted Linze, so refusing those two is out of the question. I like them all about the same. They're all important to me. I don't want to, nor do I think myself capable of doing anything to hurt them. But that's exactly what makes me question if I'm really the right person for them. I'm scared that this situation might just make them sad in the end. Or maybe I'm just scared for myself… Marriage is a big deal, after all. It isn't just my own problem. I have to shoulder the lives of other people. Being cautious is natural, isn't it? Not only that, but the burden on me is four times heavier. Can I really carry that weight?*

"Hmmm… Maybe I should consult someone."

*Leim… would surely just side with Yumina. Lapis, Cecile, Crea… I'm somewhat reluctant to discuss this with women. Renne isn't even an option. Julio… is a bit unreliable… Guess there's only one person I can count on.*

What I did next was something I'd wanted to try for a while. I just hadn't gotten the opportunity. *I don't want to just talk to Him, I should go see Him in person.*

*I went to the kitchen and took some baked sweets to bring to Him as a kind gesture. After I was done gathering bits and pieces, I held the stuff under my armpit.*

**"[Gate]."** I walked through my shining portal and was instantly greeted by an ever-expanding, shining sea of clouds. Among the clouds was an old tea table, neatly placed on a small patch of tatami mats. *Ah, now this is nostalgic.*

There was an old man sitting next to the table. He turned to me, seemingly frozen in surprise as he bit into a rice cracker.

"…O-Oh. Oh my. It seems I have a visitor. Hoho, if you were going to drop by, you should have informed me ahead of time. I'll actually be quite honest with you, though. I had no idea that you even *could* come back here of your own free will."

"It's been quite a while, God." I'd been there before, so I had the idea that maybe I could use **[Gate]** to return. I didn't actually expect it to work, though.

"This realm is dense with magic, after all. That is probably why you could come back. It is also the reason why you could not return to your previous world. The magic in the atmosphere on your Earth is very thin, I'll have you know."

"Oh, this is for you. I brought cookies and stuff."

"Oho, thank you very much. I believe that warrants a nice cup of tea." He began filling a teacup with hot water. And, of course, it turned into tea the moment it poured from the spout. But what else was I expecting? He was God.

I silently drank the warm tea.

*Ah, delicious. It's been a while since I last had green tea…*

"Well now, what brings you to my humble abode?"

"Ah, there's something I wanted to consult you about…"

"Hmm? Well, do tell." I began explaining my situation to him. I wanted to know what I had to do about my circumstances and how I should interact with the girls moving forward… I made sure to cover all the necessary details.

"Hmm… Are you not simply overthinking things? They said they love you, so why not just be happy?"

"Well, I am, but I can't help but consider all the things that come with it."

*Sharing my worries with God makes me feel like I'm at a confessional. Not like I sinned or anything, though…*

"Very well, then. Let me call in the specialist."

"Huh?" God reached for the black phone at his side and dialed a number.

A few moments later, a woman rose up from the sea of clouds. It looked like she was in her early twenties. Her hair was as pink and as fluffy as the thin, white silk she was wearing. She floated through the air toward me. Her wrists and ankles were adorned with golden rings, and her neck had a solid gold collar-piece around it. I also noticed that she wore no shoes.

"Kept you waiting, huh?" She sat at the tea table after giving a playful greeting.

"Er… and this is?"

"This lovely lady is the god of love. I thought she would be the perfect person for your troubles."

*The god of love?! Her?!*

"Well, well. Lovely to meet you! I must say, I've been watching you every now and then! You're a very interesting young man." *Now that she mentions it, God did mention something like this once before… Something about a god of love that had taken an interest in me, if I recall. So this is the woman herself? I never expected to be consulting a deity about this. God only knows, I guess.*

"So, the title 'god of love' means exactly what it says on the tin, right?"

"Yes, it does. But it's not like I control people's feelings, get it? I just do a little of this, and a little of that… things that set the mood and create those standard, love-related cliches. I guess you could say I'm the producer of situations like those!"

"Cliches…?" *Oh, I think I get what she means. She's probably referring to those cases where girls are late to school, hurry there with toast in their mouths, and run into a great guy who just happened to walk around the corner.*

"Yeah! Cliches! All the lovey-dovey ones. If you need a specific example, I'm the one who seeks out guys who go 'Darling, I swear to you… when I return from the battlefield, we will finally be married.' And then I make sure they never ever reach the altar!"

"That kind of thing is your fault?!" *By "never ever reach the altar," she clearly means that she makes them die, right?! Wait, that's a death flag, not a love flag!*

"So, what's up?" I had my reservations about consulting her, but I really had no other choice. She *happened* to be the goddess of love, so I figured maybe she would have some good advice. At any rate, I hastily explained my current situation.

"Hmm… sounds like things are getting super interesting." The god of love smiled, reached for the cookie on the table, and stuffed it into her mouth. *She's not one for manners, clearly.*

"But I still don't see your problem. It's fine if you like each other, isn't it?"

"But… four girls at the same time?"

"There's your first mistake! You have to discard the common sense of the world you used to live in! If you only love one of them and consider the others to be extras, you're not only making them pitiful, but you're also being cruel as well! But if you love them all and are truly intent on making them happy, then that's just another form of true love, get it?"

*Love... Do I even feel it for them, though?*

"Why did they even fall in love with me...?"

"I don't know! Sometimes you get the ones who fall in love at first sight, and other times there are those who don't realize their feelings because the target of their affections is too close to them. Each person has their own life, and there's a lot of room for variation there! Love doesn't fly straight like an arrow! There's many paths to it, get it?" Part of me understood her explanation, but another part of me didn't. Still, I at least understood the point that there was no true form to love.

"Interested in what I think? Seems to me that you lack confidence. You're worried about whether or not you're worthy of responding to their feelings. But here's the thing, young man! You aren't the one who decides if you're worthy. They are!"

*Damn... Kind of feels like she hit the nail on the head.* I was just feeling weird because I felt like the girls were idealizing me. I didn't believe that I fit the image of me that was in their heads.

"You should be more honest with yourself and see where these feelings lead. Sure, it's important to be considerate of how others feel, but you can't just go and act against your own interests in the process. Doing so wouldn't just be rude to yourself, but also to the girls who confessed, get it?"

"I see... So I'm allowed to be a bit selfish, then?"

"That's more like it! Love isn't about one-sided happiness! It's meaningless if you don't become happy, too."

*...That's true. I have things I can never let go of. I have to talk things out and reconcile with the girls. Those reservations might be*

*with me for the rest of my life, but at the very least, I have to get them to agree to that.*

"Did you find your answer?" God spoke up as if he just read my mind.

"I'm not sure, but I think it's in sight at least."

"Very well, then. That is quite good to know."

"Eheh, glad to see the cliche I granted you didn't go to waste!"

*…Hm? She said something strange just now… Cliche? One of the things she manufactures, right?*

"What exactly do you mean by that? The cliche you granted me, I mean."

"Oh, just a little while ago, I produced a situation in which you walked in on them changing and then got really surprised. You should be thanking me, get it?"

"That was you?!" *This god of love seems to be a fan of generic scenarios.*


In the evening, I had the girls gather in the living room. Laim, Lapis, and the others weren't with us. It was only myself and the four girls who had confessed.

The four sat on the couch in front me and patiently waited for my words.

I considered all of those girls far too good for me. That was exactly why I didn't want to lie to them and wished to let them know my true feelings.

"Alright, well, to start things off let me just say… I have no plans of getting married."

**"WHHHAAAATTT?!!"** The four of them leaped off the couch at the same time. Their surprise took verbal form and echoed throughout the living room.

"Wait, what?!"

"H-Have we done something wrong, have we?"

"…You said you'd accept me as your wife…"

"Touya?!" All four girls leaped to their feet at once and closed in on me. *Crap, that came out wrong!*

"Okay, wait! I only meant 'right now,' all right! I wanted to say that I've got no plans of getting married *right now*!" My words stopped the girls dead in their tracks. *Okay, good. They're at least willing to hear me out.*

"If not right now, then at some point in the future?"

"Of course. If none of you are against the idea, I'll marry all four of you quite happily." I answered Elze's question, and the girls returned to their seats. *Good, they've calmed down a bit…*

"I like all of you equally, and I don't plan on breaking my promise to marry you, but I can't get married right now. I don't want it to feel like we're only together because I got caught up in the moment."

"…I do not understand what you mean, I do not." Yae tilted her head in confusion.

"What I mean is, I just don't think I'm ready for a commitment like that yet. I'm not mature enough to look after other people. I mean, I'm still not fully convinced I can even look after *myself* at the moment. So, please, wait until I *am* ready to carry the weight of another life alongside my own. If it doesn't seem like I'll ever become that sort of person, you're free to leave my side at any moment. Nobody can take that right away from you; not me or anyone else." That was my own selfish condition to the agreement. I wanted everyone to be happy, but I wasn't yet sure if I could *make* them happy. I was still lacking in so many areas. I didn't have the resolve, the courage, the strong feelings of love, or the knowledge to make any of them happy just yet.

I knew that I was basically just telling the girls to wait until I felt like I was worthy of them, but I didn't intend to just lead them on indefinitely until I suddenly decided that day had come. The condition I'd laid out for them could've easily made any girl hate me, and I could've accepted it if any of them decided to call the whole thing off for that reason alone. That was their choice to make, and I intended to respect their wishes.

"...You really couldn't have worded that any better? I mean, I guess that makes sense, but still." Elze sighed as she spoke, with an expression that was somewhere between exasperation and relief. Hell, the fact of the matter was that the girls had all proposed to me, and what I had said was just as bad as if I'd never said anything at all. I was unsure of what to do. I would basically be taking away their choices in the matter for my own convenience. Even *I* felt like that was a horrible thing to do to someone.

"You're playing dirty. You already know that we'd never just throw you aside like that, but you're pretending like we have that option anyway, right?" Elze shot another glare at me as she spoke. *Well, I mean, I don't think that highly of myself, but it's not like I was expecting you all to just cut all ties with me here and now or anything.*

"Falling in love is never an easy thing, it is not..." Yae gave Elze a pat on the shoulder. Elze herself turned her head away and puffed up her cheeks.

"...Even if my sister gives up on you, Touya, I'll wait for as long as I have to... Because I want to be your wife."

"Hey, who said anything about me giving up on him?!" Linze laughed as she watched her sister panic. *Oh good, she was just teasing her.*

"I'm fine with that, too. We've already talked this over among ourselves, after all. Now all we have to do is make you fall so completely head-over-heels in love with us that you'll be the one proposing to *us* next time."

"Guess I'll just have to do my best to keep you from falling out of love with me before then." Yumina's words brought a smile to my face. *From now on, we're not just party members anymore. I'm engaged to these girls. They're my lovers, and one day we'll all be part of the same family. I need to do my best so that day comes even a little sooner, and when it does, I'll be the one to propose to them properly.*

"So with that, all four of us are Touya's fiancées. Shall we line up in order and have him kiss us as proof?"

"WHAT?!" Elze, Linze, Yae, and I were all caught completely off-guard by Yumina's abrupt suggestion. Meanwhile, it looked like she wanted to give herself a pat on the back for coming up with such a cunning plan. *Why are you never satisfied with things getting wrapped up semi-normally for a change?!*

"W-Wait, umm, d-don't you think it's still a bit too soon for that?!"

"Th-Though we may be e-engaged now, I do believe we should take things in due moderation, we should…!" Elze turned red as a tomato and broke out in a panic. Yae was bright red, too. While I could understand Yae's reaction, I wouldn't have taken Elze to be such a late bloomer.

"But he kissed me just yesterday, you know?"

"Huh?!" As Yumina muttered those words, Elze and Yae turned their heads in my direction with such speed that I worried they might get whiplash. *I mean, she's not lying, but, uh…*

"A-Actually, he k-kissed me, too… On the forehead, I mean…"

"HUH?!" Linze spoke up, and this time the two turned to face me with even greater speed than before. *I mean, she's not lying either, but give me a break here!*

"A-Alright then, that settles it! You've gotta k-k-k-kiss us, too!"

"I would… like a kiss, too, I would…"

*Alright, hold up! Aren't you the very same girls who were just saying that it was "too soon" or that we should "take things in moderation" a second ago? What part of this is "moderate" to you?!* Elze and Yae locked me down with their gazes, still blushing up to their ears.

*Crap, I can't exactly run away now… Not after I just decided I'd accept everything about them.*

I reached out my hand and drew Elze closer toward me. She jumped a little at my touch, but she didn't put up any resistance as I gently pulled her body in. I placed my hand on her cheek, then drew my face closer to hers, when…

"T-Too embarrassing, changed my mind!"

"Ghuoh?!" Leaving me with only those words, Elze's fist came crashing directly into my solar plexus without warning. The abrupt force gave me no time to steel myself, so I collapsed for the second time that day. As my consciousness faded, the only thought to cross my mind was something along the lines of *oh no, not again…*


"…Ungh?"

"Have you regained consciousness?" I awoke to find myself back in my own room, lying on my bed. The sun had long since set.

Through the dim lamp-light, I could make out the figure of Cesca sitting in a chair next to my bed. She was dressed in a maid uniform, for some reason.

"Cesca…? What's with those clothes…?"

"Lady Lapis presented me with them. If I am to serve my Master, then this is to be my uniform, so I have been instructed."

…*Come to think of it, I just kind of left Cesca in the maids' hands the minute we got back home, huh? I didn't forget about her or anything, but too many life-changing decisions kept flying at me one after another, and… Hang on, that's all this girl's fault, anyway!*

"Alright, but what brings you to my bedroom?"

"I have come to make love to you." I leaped to the edge of my bed like I'd just heard a gunshot fire in my direction. The fog in my mind cleared itself up instantly. *My chastity is in danger!*

"That was a joke. I have no plans for that. Not today." *Don't just casually stick "not today" on the end like you think I won't notice! I can never let my guard down around you for even a second!*

"The truth is that I've come to deliver a message addressed to you."

"A message for me…? Who's it from?"

"It is from Doctor Regina Babylon." *Hold the phone, what? A message for me… from that ancient genius doc? The very same person who created Cesca and the Hanging Garden of Babylon?! But how?* Cesca moved her right hand to her left wrist as if to take her own pulse, only to open her left wrist up and bring out a cable with some sort of connector on the end.

"Whoa." *It's times like these that I have to remind myself that Cesca's actually a machine.*

Cesca took the cable and presented the end of it to me.

"Huh? What am I supposed to do with this?"

"I am unsure. The doctor told me that if I gave this to my new Master, then he would understand." *Instructions unclear. Unfortunately, as a flesh-and-blood human being, I can't think of any other places that I could comfortably "connect" a thing like that to... Do I stick it in my mouth...? Wait, could it be? The shape of this connector looks familiar, but... No, that can't be right!*

I went over to where my coat was hanging up on the wall, then took my smartphone out of the pocket. After that, I took the cable Cesca had offered to me and tried plugging it in. It fit perfectly.

My phone made a little beeping noise when it picked up the foreign cable, and the screen displayed a loading bar that slowly filled up with green. When the loading bar hit 100%, my smartphone's screen suddenly lit up brightly.

"H-Hey, what is this?!" The light gradually died down to reveal a person roughly 15 centimeters in height standing on top of the screen.

The person was semi-transparent, almost as if to assure me that I was merely seeing a 3D projected image... which would have been fine, except my phone wasn't even capable of projecting holograms, to my knowledge.

The holographic person was a lady who looked to be in her early twenties. She wore a white lab coat and glasses, and had what looked like a cigarette in her mouth. Her long, blonde hair hung down messily, which I felt was a shame because it would've suited her perfectly otherwise. The top and skirt that she wore beneath her lab coat were also creased, adding to her overall slovenly appearance.

"This is Doctor Regina Babylon."

"This is the doctor...?" The doctor, who had until then been sitting somewhat listlessly, turned her face up to gaze at mine as she grinned at me. *Huh?*

"Howdy there. Nice to meetcha, kid. The name's Regina Babylon, as you know. Before anything else, let me just thank you for taking up administration of the garden, as well as Francesca. Really, it means a lot to me, *Mochizuki Touya*."

"Wait, how did you...?" *What does this mean? Why does someone from almost five thousand years ago know my name?! Not just that, but why does this connector fit into my smartphone perfectly? It's almost as if it was specifically designed to be used exactly like that from the very beginning...*

"Trust me, I know how you feel. I mean, that's a very good question. Of course you'd want to know. After all, you're a very special kind of person."

*Special...? Wait, does she know that I'm from another world?! Just who is this Doctor, anyway?!*

"Allow me to give you the answer you so long for. Look closely now." The doctor spoke slowly, and as she did, she raised her skirt up before my eyes. Black lace panties consumed my vision.

"This is my favorite pair, I'll have you know."

"The hell do I care?!" I threw my smartphone down onto my bed without thinking. *The hell do you mean I'm "that kind of person"?! Don't just lump me in with you! It's not like your panties were the first thing I wanted to know about or anything, alright?!*

"Ha ha ha! I'm kidding, I'm only kidding. Don't worry about it, that was just my way of breaking the ice." Or so the good doctor said, still attempting to flash her panties at me from her new position atop the bed, grinning at me all the while. *I knew it, this person's way beyond your regular eccentric!* The holographic doctor returned her cigarette-like object to her lips, that grin never leaving her face.

"I'll explain everything to you, so forgive my little prank. Firstly, why do I know about you? Well, you see, I have a device that allows me to glimpse into the future." *A device for looking into the future? Is it some kind of Artifact? I had no idea she was such a genius that she could even make something like that... She's still a weirdo, though.*

"I mixed a bit of Space-Time Magic together with some Light magic, and then used a Null spell called... Well, never mind. That's not important. What's important is that I made a device that can project the future. The problem is, the device has a couple of fatal flaws. First, the visions of the future I can observe are only fragmentary, and second, I don't get to decide how far into the future I want to look. The device seeks out someone with the same biorhythm as the wielder from the future, and proceeds to reflect events from that person's life. In my case, having an affinity for all the base magic elements came back to bite me, meaning the extremely far-off future that *you* are in is the only one I've been able to get a look at." *You're telling me I have the same biorhythm as this nutty professor? I don't even know what that means, but I don't like it. It feels like she's lumping me in with her as partners in crime or something... I'm not like that, okay?! We might be the same kind of person, but that only extends as far as our magical alignments, got it?!*

"Anyway, that's how I caught sight of you. At first I was only looking out of curiosity, but then things got more and more fun as time went by. It got to the point where I was having great fun watching you and your party go about your wild adventures, but then one day, I wasn't able to see your future anymore. Why do you think that was? It's because the future had changed. No, that's not quite the right word for it. I suppose a better way to put it would be that your future became *uncertain*." *Uncertain...? What's an uncertain future mean?*

α (The past) ——————————— β (The future)

**Let's imagine time moving in a straight line from past to future, like this. If, somewhere along the line from α to β, an unknown factor named γ were to intervene, then the new future would change from β to β1.**

**If the future the doctor had been looking at so far was future β, then some huge event big enough to change the future, Event γ, must have happened, creating future β1 as a new possibility... I think.**

"I thought it might have been the fall of Partheno... but that event is likely already set in stone. After all, our civilization doesn't exist in your world anymore. Anyway, the fall of Partheno was brought about by the enemy of mankind, the Phrase, and their relentless invasion. That much was already an established fact in your era, too." *The Phrase... Wait, the Phrase?! The crystal creatures that Leen told me about! So the fall of the five-thousand-year-old civilization was brought about by that same weird species?!*

"We fought back, of course, but the Phrase came at us in the tens of thousands. Nothing could be done to prevent the fall of Partheno. After that, the Phrase scattered to all corners of the world. It was truly the end of days. I'm sure that the reason I stopped being able to see the future beyond that point is simply that there *is* no future for the world under those circumstances."

**So the flow of events between α (The past that the doctor existed in) and β (The future that I'm currently inhabiting) was slowly tilting toward β1 (The future where the Phrase destroyed the world)? But still, that doesn't make too much sense. The world is fine.**

"Right. As I'm sure you've noticed, your future never came to an end. For some reason, they disappeared from the world before the worst possible outcome could occur. I don't know how or why, but thanks to their abrupt disappearance, I was able to see the future you inhabit once more."

*That means β1 was ultimately averted. That's good to know, at least. If β1 had been the future of this world instead of β, God might've sent me somewhere else entirely, and then I wouldn't have been able to meet with everyone here.*

*Still, what could've made the Phrase just up and vanish from the world one day…? Were they wiped out by some kind of Phrase-targeting virus like in some sci-fi novel or something?*

"Anyway, that should suffice as an explanation as to why I know *all* about you. And naturally, I left Babylon there as a little present for you. Use it however you like. I've even filled it with lovely girls catered to your tastes. Feel free to use *them* however you like, too!" The holographic doctor gave me an evil little smirk when she said that. *Dammit, what's with this feeling?! Her whole face is just saying "No, no, don't worry. I understand perfectly. You're a boy, I get how it is," and it's driving me up the wall! This must be what it feels like to have an older sister who gets her kicks out of messing with you!*

"Just in case, I split Babylon up into multiple parts to prevent it from falling into the wrong hands. Whether you go hunting for the rest of the pieces or not is up to you, I don't mind either way. It all belongs to you now, anyway. From what I've seen, it doesn't really seem like you'll be needing anything so absurdly powerful in your future, anyhow."

*Then why did you even build it?! I know they say the line between genius and stupidity is paper thin, but this person's clearly way over that line!*

"Well, I've been talking for a while now, so I'll end the message around here. Oh, and by the way, when this message finishes playing, Francesca will strip naked."

"Whhhat?!"

"That was a joke. Anyway, see you around, kid."

I threw my smartphone at the bed again. *Ugh! Goddammit, that little Doctor Panties kept making fun of me right till the end! I don't get her at all! Did she seriously build all of Babylon for the sole purpose of messing with a kid five thousand years in the future?!*

"…Shall I strip?"

"Thou shalt not strip!" I quickly stayed Cesca's hand.

So the long and short of it was, Doctor Babylon had been peeking in on us from the past, so she knew all about us. But if she really could see the future, then why was the teleportation circle for the garden located at the bottom of the sea off the coast of Eashen? For that matter, why bother splitting Babylon into several pieces if she knew it was going to me, anyway? It made it all very hard to believe she was seeing the future perfectly.

*No, wait. She said she could only take fragmentary glances into the future, so maybe she couldn't zoom in on the finer details or something. I really hope that's the case, because if it's not, then I'll never be able to rest easy again knowing that someone's peeking in on everything I'm doing all the time.*

Another thing that caught my attention was the Phrase. From how she spoke, it seemed like the Doctor *wasn't aware* that the Phrase still existed in this world line.

*Maybe that cricket-type Phrase we met at the old capital had actually just been sealed there this entire time. If so, it would mean that the Phrase invaded one thousand years ago, too... That would explain why the old capital came to ruin so suddenly, and why it had to be relocated in the first place. It all makes sense if I consider all these events to be related.*

*So if the one that we ran into was probably a survivor from when the old capital was invaded, then... I'd bet it was originally caught so that people could research it to try and find some kind of weak point.*

*But hang on... If that were the case for the cricket-shaped one, then what about the snake-shaped one that Leen saw? Shouldn't we take this as a sign that the events that happened five-thousand years ago, and then more recently one-thousand years ago, are about to happen all over again?*

Five-thousand years ago, the world was on the brink of destruction. One-thousand years ago, the old capital fell. Following that pattern, the events appeared to be reducing in scale. Even if it were to happen again, things likely wouldn't turn out as disastrous as the last couple of times... Still, it would've been foolish to make that assumption.

"Is something the matter?"

"Nah, it's nothing…"

*This is all just "what if" right now. If my fears turn out to be unfounded, then I couldn't ask for anything more, but on the off-chance that my guess is right…*

"Won't do me any good to keep dwelling on it, I suppose. I'm sure it'd just make everyone feel uneasy, so I'll keep quiet about it."

"About my making love to you?"

"You'll do no such thing, and that is *not* what I meant!"

"Understood, Master." This train of events could have easily spiraled out of control. The last thing I wanted to deal with immediately after getting engaged was being accused of cheating. I chased Cesca away, since I'd already made sure that she'd been given her own room, and crawled into bed.

The next day, I paid a visit to the shopping district in the southern part of the capital.

My destination was a jeweler's. I figured I should, you know, buy engagement rings for everyone.

I could've easily made the rings myself using [**Modeling**], but cheaping out on an important gift to one's fiancee just felt wrong to me, so I wanted to buy them from the store instead. That said, I had no idea what the going price for engagement rings even was. I'd heard before that an engagement ring was normally "three months' wages," but I'd also heard that *that* was just a rumor spread by jewelers to make people spend more on them. Not that it mattered either way, since I wasn't even being paid in "wages" in this world…

From what I'd read online, an engagement ring was something a guy gave to a girl upon getting engaged. This was the one that was supposed to cost "three months' wages." And then separate from that, there was the pair of rings exchanged during a wedding and then worn all the time by a husband and wife. Because these rings were left on all the time, they didn't have to be overly expensive, apparently. It also seemed to be the norm for wedding rings to come without jewels attached.

For a normal wedding, I'd only need to buy three rings. One engagement ring, a wedding ring for my wife, and a wedding ring for me, but in my case I had four wives, so I'd ultimately need four engagement rings for the girls, four wedding rings for the girls, and a wedding ring for myself, for a total of nine rings...

*Hang on, is that even how weddings work over here? I only just noticed, but that's just a custom from my world. I don't even know if things work that way over here. I mean, wedding rings are probably the norm at least, but...*

Unsure of the local customs, I decided to ask the person who worked in the jewelry shop when I got there.

As I walked through the shopping district with my head full of such thoughts, I happened to overhear an argument going on. Curious to see what kind of trouble was brewing, I went over toward the food stall that the voices were coming from. When I got there, I found the stall manager standing with his arms crossed, angrily eyeing the customer in front.

"Look, kid. I don't know where ya got them coins or what they're worth, and I don't really care. Ya can't pay with them here. We don't take 'em. Capisce?"

"That's troublesome. I'm afraid these are all I have, you see..." The customer was a boy around the same age as me. He wore a black top over a white shirt, black pants, and had a long white scarf around his neck. His color scheme was perfectly monotone. He stood there scratching his head, clearly troubled. Even the hair he was scratching at on his head was pure white. In his hands he held two crepes, one half-eaten.

"Eeehh, can't I just pay with this, though? This is money too, you know?"

"If you don't got any money, then that's the same as stealing my food. Don't make me hand you over to the guards, kid. I'm tellin' ya, we don't got no weird coins like that in this country!"

"Uhh, excuse me…" I couldn't help but stick my nose in. From what I could gather, it seemed the boy didn't have any of this country's currency, but he went and accidentally took a bite out of some food without realizing that he wouldn't be able to pay for it.

"Yeah? Whaddya want?" The shopkeeper barked at me angrily.

"I'm just passing through, but if it's just about the money, then I can pay for his share. Would that be alright?"

"I ain't complainin', just so long as yer payin'." I handed the man one copper coin, and he gave me two more crepes. Four crepes for one copper seemed a reasonably decent price. With that matter sorted, the boy and I left the stand with food in hand.

"Thanks. You really helped me out of a bind there."

"Don't worry about it, really. But I've gotta ask, do you really not have any money you can use around these parts? Like, none at all?" The boy thanked me, and I had to check with him just to make sure. I couldn't help but wonder where in the world he'd come from. After all, even Eashen used the same common currency as Belfast, and those places were almost on the opposite sides of the world.

"See, I was able to buy stuff with this money before, though…" The scarf-clad boy took a handful of silver coins out of his pocket.

"They've got a pretty weird shape to them." The common currency in this world was chiefly round as far as I understood it. This was true for gold, silver, and all other types of coin. In comparison, the coins the boy was holding were 8-sided. They were octagonal-shaped coins. I'd never seen their kind before. I picked one up out of his hand so that I could examine both sides properly.

"If they've caught your eye, then I'll give you a few as thanks for earlier. It doesn't seem like I'll be able to use them here, anyway."

"You sure? Alright, I guess I'll take just enough to cover the cost of the crepes, then." Honestly I didn't really want them *that* much, but I figured accepting his offer would keep him from getting hung up over it, so I took a few of the coins from him.

"My name's Touya. Mochizuki Touya. What's yours?"

"Ende. It's a pleasure, Touya." He extended his hand, and I gripped it in a firm handshake. I remembered thinking at the time how unnaturally cold his skin felt. That was a fateful day, the event that served as the first meeting between myself and the boy named Ende.

"Hmm, what should I do? It's gonna be tough not having any money." Ende tilted his head while eating his crepe. I bit into mine, too, and we gazed on at the crowds of people coming and going in front of the water fountain.

"Yeah, no kidding. You're probably just gonna have to get a job for now."

"What's your job, Touya?"

"Mine?" *My job... My job, huh? I've never thought about it much before, but what is my job, exactly? Adventurer, I guess? I mean, technically most of my work is done through the guild and all.*

"I do odd jobs here and there as an adventurer with the guild. You know, stuff like hunting monsters or guarding caravans."

"Ah, I see. Sounds like something that'd work for me." *You make it sound so simple. Well, I guess there's no massive risks of danger at the lower ranks, so it should be fine.*

"You thinking about getting registered? What are you gonna do about getting a weapon? Well, you could always just do plant-gathering quests for the time being, I guess."

"Why would I need a weapon? It's not like I'm going to be off slaying Dragons, right?" *Is he planning on going at it barehanded? Is he a brawler like Elze? Then again, he could also be a mage.* Something caught me about the way he had said that, though. Almost as if he was saying that even Dragons would've been a piece of cake for him if he had a weapon.

"Well, alright. I can lead you to the guild office, then. I had some business there today, anyway."

"Please do. Sorry for all the trouble." I threw the empty crepe wrappers in the garbage and made my way over to the Guild. I needed to withdraw money to buy the rings for the girls, after all.

Ende was a little bit taller than me. Around 170 centimeters, give or take. His looks were fairly androgynous, too, like one of those pretty-boy characters. *Damn it, I'm not jealous or anything, you hear me?!*

My eyes couldn't help but be drawn to his white scarf, how it trailed almost all the way to the ground. It wasn't even winter, so I had no idea why he needed such a long scarf anyway.

"It was a gift from someone precious to me." When I inquired about it, that was how he answered with a smile on his face. He kind of missed my point, though. Did he mean that his girlfriend gave it to him? His tone of voice sure made it seem so. The guild's sign came into sight before too long. The hustle and bustle around the quest board was as lively as ever.

I took Ende up to the counter and had the receptionist run him through the registration process. While he was busy with that, I went to withdraw some money from the adjacent counter. This was a once-in-a-lifetime thing, or so I wanted to believe, so I wanted to splurge on the rings.

When we met back up, I had my money ready and Ende had his brand new Black guild card in hand.

"No troubles with your registration, then?"

"Went just fine. All that's left now is to start doing quests. I didn't know the guild had offices all around the world, though. That saves me a lot of trouble. I'm never in one place for very long." *That so,* I thought. For a traveler, he sure was dressed rather lightly. Hell, I was impressed he'd been able to make it so far as a traveler with no usable money to his name. He had this sort of blissfully ignorant air about him, too. I thought for a moment that maybe he was some runaway prince from a distant land.

I had my suspicions about the guy, but I decided not to pry. Everyone had their own circumstances, after all.

"Well, I should really get going. Try and stick to the simpler quests at first, yeah? Don't push yourself too hard now."

"Got it. Thanks for everything, Touya. Hope we meet again somewhere."

"Yeah, I'll see you around." I parted ways with Ende and left the guild office. He really was an odd one.

With that out of the way, I made for the jewelers.

Each of the four girls in front of me sat with their rings, and gazed at them with great big smiles on their faces. Their design was a fairly simple platinum band with a diamond on each, but they still cost me a pretty penny. Looking back on it, from the moment I told the lady that I didn't know the standard price for these things, I should've expected that she'd try to overcharge me. I mean, once I'd decided on a design and heard the cost, I asked for four of them and the lady's eyes went wide.

The rings I'd chosen were enchanted ones, with a spell that let them naturally adjust to the size of the wearer's finger. In addition to that, I'd included some enchantments of my own.

"Each of those is enchanted with [**Accel**], [**Transfer**], and [**Storage**], by the way." I figured [**Accel**] was a good battle choice, [**Transfer**] would let the rings work as spare magic batteries in case they ever ran out at a critical moment, and [**Storage**] would be a handy spell for any girl to have.

"Thank you so much, Touya." Yumina held her left hand in her right, and smiled as she gazed down at the ring on her finger.

Next up, I took out a mithril chain necklace.

"Here, Elze. This is for you."

"For me?" Elze took the chain, seemingly a little puzzled.

"Well you can't really wear that ring under a gauntlet, right? I figured a necklace would let you keep it on even if we got into any fights."

"Oh, gotcha. I never thought of that. Thanks, Touya." Elze put the ring on the chain and wore it around her neck to see how it looked. I felt it really suited her. Since the chain was mithril, there was no chance of it breaking, and as long as the ring was somewhere on Elze's person she'd be able to make use of the magic it'd been enchanted with.

With the rings handed over, I realized I still had something in my pockets. I reached in and took out the silver coins that Ende had given me, and placed them down on the table.

"What are these?"

"Earlier today I met this weird guy called Ende, and I got these from him. Apparently they're some country's currency. Recognize them at all?" Linze took one of the coins and began inspecting it with great interest.

"I've never seen anything like this before… They have a very elaborate design carved into them, so I can only imagine that they're considerably valuable…" I sure hoped that wasn't the case, because I'd basically taken them as payment for two whole crepes. I began to wonder if maybe taking Ende to get them converted into usable currency would have been the better idea. Thinking about it, even just taking him to a pawn shop would've gotten him at least the price of the silver they were made of.

I took one of the coins and gave it another good look over for myself. I heard a knock at the door, and Renne popped her head into the room. She held the door open for Cesca, who brought with her a teapot and some cups.

"I've come to serve you tea." Cesca said, as she placed the cups onto the table and began to pour tea for us. As I was watching her do that, Renne came up beside me acting all fidgety. It looked like she had something to say. *I wonder what's up…*

"Um, Touya… er, sir. Can I getcha to… Um, I mean, I do indeed have a request, sir…"

"You don't have to force yourself to speak politely when Leim's not around. What's up?"

"Well, y'see, I wanna ride a bike, too…" *A bike? I guess I don't really see anything wrong with that. I dunno how I'd feel about her riding it around town, but it should be fine if she's got someone with her at the time.*

"I wanna practice, but my feet don't reach the danged pedals! Sue said you made a littler bike for her before, and, uhhm…" *Aha, now I get it. The only bike we have at home is an adult-sized one. Renne's still too small to ride a bike like that. I should've noticed without her having to point it out to me.*

"No problem, Renne! I'll make one especially for you, then. What color would you like?"

"Really? Yer not havin' a laugh?! Then… a red one!"

"Your wish is my command, little lady."

"That's spot-on! Thanks a bunch!" Renne leaned across the sofa and hugged me tight. *C'mon now, if Leim were here he'd be furious, you know? Still, I'm just happy if you're happy.*

I wore an awkward little smile and just let Renne hug me, when my eyes met with Cesca's.

"…So you're a pedoph—"

**"Hey there, nice weather we're having today, am I right?!"** *I can't let you finish that word, Tin Can! I'm already self-conscious enough about that kind of thing thanks to Yumina, so don't make this any worse for me!* Cesca gave me a suspicious stare for a while, but eventually went back to pouring tea like the little outburst had never happened. After she was done, she caught notice of the coins laying on the table and tilted her head slightly.

"I didn't think this currency would still be in use after all this time."

"What do you mean, after all this time? Cesca, you know where these came from?"

"Yes. These particular coins are Partheno Silver. They were first minted exactly five thousand two hundred and eighty four years ago, and were used commonly around this region, too. I'm amazed that they're still in circulation." *That long ago?!* Cesca's words made me pick the coin up once more and examine it even more intently. It definitely didn't look that old in the slightest. Hell, it looked almost brand new. Why would Ende have been carrying something like this around...? *Hang on. What was it he said back then?*

"See, I was able to buy stuff with this money before, though..."

*Before? What did he mean by "before," exactly? Is there really anywhere in the world that might still be using a currency from the days of old?* I had an idea, but it was a ridiculous one. It almost seemed to me as though Ende was a human who had time traveled here from the past. Either that, or he could have been one of Doctor Babylon's android creations like Cesca.

"Cesca, out of curiosity, were there any males among those of you made by Doctor Babylon?"

"Males...? No, none at all. The doctor never bothered making any males. There were a few with more masculine personalities, however."

*More masculine, huh... Come to think of it, Ende did strike me as rather androgynous. Looking back, I can't really say for sure that Ende's really a "he" at all. I mean, I highly doubt that's the case, but...* Cesca watched as I became lost in thought and shot me an even more suspicious glance. *What is it this time?*

"...So you're a homos—"

"Alrighty, that's enough! Stop! Please, for the love of God, don't go there!" *That's not what I was asking, and I certainly don't swing that way! I'm straight as a ruler! Man, I just really love girls!!!*

"Do not worry, Master. Be it young boys or big, burly-armed men, I will try to adjust myself to better suit your tastes. Shall I wear short shorts from now on?"

"Thou shalt not!" *Man, why is she strangely knowledgeable about these things in particular? Is she just taking after her creator like kids take after their parents? Look. Go on, look at what you've done. Everyone's confused now... Except for Linze. Why's she blushing?*

The next day, we all headed off to the guild. I was thinking that maybe I'd be able to meet with Ende again, but I also thought that it'd be nice to raise our guild rank to the next tier.

Yumina was Green, one step behind the rest of us, who were Blue. The ranking system worked in an ascending order; Black, Purple, Green, Blue, Red, Silver, and then Gold. I wanted to get up to Red, because then I'd be considered a veteran adventurer.

We had already struck down a Black Dragon, which was the kind of thing that would've corresponded to a Red Rank deed if we had done it through the guild's quest board. In short, we definitely had what it took.

Plus, the bigger the jobs, the bigger the payout. I was still unsure about exactly what it was I wanted to do, but I knew I'd need cash regardless. I was betrothed now, after all. I had to become more responsible.

Everyone was quite familiar with Kohaku at this point, but it seemed that Kokuyou and Sango were drawing quite a bit of attention with their swimming-through-the-air routine.

«The two of you should've stayed back at home. You're far too conspicuous.»

«Poppycock! Where our good lord goes, I shall follow.»

«Exactly. Bessidess, don't you ssstick out jusst asss much asss we do, Kohaku?» The three of them spoke through the telepathic link, but I could clearly hear everything. To be honest, the only reason they were sticking out so much was because of their floating. It could easily be remedied if they'd just let me carry them. But, when I offered, they refused.

They said it was a matter of personal pride, and that they couldn't accept being carried around by me. Well, it wasn't a huge deal. I decided that if anyone asked about their air-swimming, I'd just say "a wizard did it."

When we finally made it into the guild, I looked around, but I couldn't see Ende anywhere in the crowd. I wondered if he'd already gone to another town.

While everyone else went to check out the request board, I caught the attention of the receptionist that I had signed up Ende with yesterday. I figured I'd ask if he'd done much since then.

"Ah, the boy with the scarf? Yes, he completed a monster hunting quest yesterday and was paid quite handsomely. He was hunting Lone-Horned Wolves, I believe." *Lone-Horned Wolves, eh... That means he's progressing like a regular Black Rank should. Heh, that was one of my newbie quests, too...*

"Although..." sighed the receptionist.

"Hm? Did something happen?" The receptionist had a clearly forced smile on her face, but she couldn't hide the glint of trouble in her eyes. I wondered what Ende had done.

"His hunting quest stipulated that he must bring proof of defeat for five Lone-Horned Wolves... but he went a step further than that..."

"...You've gotta bring in a horn as proof, right? How many did he have?"

"Well, I'm not entirely sure, but it was well over fifty."

"Over fifty horns?!" I couldn't contain my surprise. Talk about overkill.

"The request was only for five, so he received the standard payment, but he sold the other horns at their going market rate. He was certainly proud of himself." *Over fifty... what a guy. Come to think of it, wasn't he unarmed? Guess he's a mage after all, then... At least that's the only way I can rationalize the massacre.*

...Well, I had no idea and there was no point dwelling on it. It wasn't my style to butt into other people's business anyway.

I decided to head toward the quest board, and the four girls who were waiting there.

"So, find anything good?"

"Ah, Touya... We did see this one, but..." Yumina pointed toward a Red Rank quest on the board. *Hmm? We can only take quests up to Blue Rank, can't we? This one's a notch above us.*

I decided to read the notice anyway.

"Mithril... Golem? What is that, a Golem made of mithril? Located in the Melicia Mountain Range... and a reward of five platinum coins? Isn't that a little cheap for a Red quest?"

"It is a tad low, yes, but that's because the foe is a Mithril Golem. Its body is a very precious material, an extremely valuable one at that. Depending on the chunks that you manage to salvage, it can sell at an exceptionally high price." That made sense to me. So in effect, the monster itself was the reward. That was quite the juicy scoop... But it wasn't like we could accept this quest anyway... or could we?

"Any adventurer with a B-Rank title or higher is permitted to take this quest, bypassing rank restrictions?" *Title...? Like the Dragon Slayer title I received a while back? As far as I understand it, there are other titles like Demon Killer and Griffin Buster.*

"Dragon Slayer is an A-Rank title, so that means..."

"Hm? We can take this quest after all?" I tore off the quest form and brought it to the front desk. *Come to think of it, while most of us have it, Yumina doesn't have the Dragon Slayer title... Are we gonna be able to take this as a group, or not?*

A low rank wasn't necessarily a great indicator of personal skill, anyway. A veteran soldier with brilliant battle prowess could always just decide to take a career change and start at the bottom ranks in the adventurer's guild, after all. Holding a title was an easy way to get recognition independent of your guild rank.

"No worries, the majority of your party hold the title, so you may take the quest as a group. Would you like to learn more?"

"Yes, please." The quest was at the base of the Melicia Mountain Range. A group working out of Stael Mine could no longer continue their excavation efforts due to a Mithril Golem settling in the middle of their operation.

The creature seemed to have exceptionally tough armor. Furthermore, it was abnormally fast for a Golem due to its material composition. It was made of mithril, so it was both lightweight and sturdy. It seemed as though many miners had already fallen victim to its rampage.

Golems were viciously territorial, so they wouldn't allow anyone to intrude on their territory. That was one of the reasons Golems were the preferred method of defense for mages and their treasure hordes.

"Well, those are the details... You guys wanna take this?" I figured I should confirm with everyone, but we all unanimously agreed. The part that needed to be destroyed was the Golem Nucleus. Apparently when that thing was trashed, the Golem couldn't maintain its form and would die out. It would be pretty hard to reach the middle of the damn thing though, since Golems were sturdy and all. A mithril one even more so.

"Couldn't we just make this another sure-win with your [**Apport**] spell? It worked last time." Elze brought up an interesting idea as soon as we left the guild, but it didn't seem feasible to me. Unlike the Phrase, the Golem wouldn't be transparent, so the nucleus wouldn't be on display. It wouldn't work on the Golem, that'd be too easy. Linze seemed to have the same idea, and she quickly shot down her sister's hope.

"A Golem Nucleus is about… this big. [**Apport**] wouldn't be able to seize something of that size." Linze held her hands out and mimed the shape of a volleyball. She was right. [**Apport**] was a spell that only worked on something you could grasp in one hand. Things of a large size were off-limits.

Seems we had no choice but to confront it head-on… It definitely wouldn't be easy. Up until that point, the Phrase had been my toughest foe, but perhaps the Golem would give it a run for its money. Well, I'd be more than happy fighting a Golem instead of something that could regenerate itself.

Linze had destructive magic like [**Explosion**] and [**Bubble Bomb**], which would surely come in handy. Yumina had the Earth spell [**Rock Crash**] as well, and that could also prove valuable.

Plus, Elze and her damage-bolstering right gauntlet would definitely be able to keep the pressure on the enemy. The only issue I could think of was Yae. She only had slashing attacks with her blades. She was fundamentally ill-equipped to deal with hardened foes.

"Fret not, I will act as a diversion this time, I will." I made a mental note to use some of the mithril to have a new katana forged for her after we finished the quest.

"So, how do we get to the Melicia Mountains? We gonna rent a carriage again? Or maybe we should just buy our own already." Elze raised a fair point. Traveling by carriage would definitely be the comfiest method, but I had another idea in mind. After all, I had gone through a lot to obtain this new mode of transportation.

"We're about to depart. Please remain in your seats until the seatbelt light has turned off."

"There are no seats. Or seatbelt lights."

"This kind of talk is necessary to the aesthetic. Please learn how to read the mood, Master." It took a few days, but it was worth having the Hanging Garden of Babylon move to the skies above Belfast. We'd be able to go anywhere we wanted in a matter of hours if we flew there on it.

We were currently around two hundred meters up in the air. We weren't even as high as the Tokyo Tower, but it was just fine due to the general lack of large structures and mountains in the area. Plus, we had a stealth field up, so nobody could even see us. The stealth field really was amazing. We didn't even cast a shadow due to it. I had no idea how that was possible, but just wrote it off as another application of lost ancient magic.

"Estimated arrival; one hour." Cesca was monitoring the central control panel in the middle of the garden, and she told me how much longer our ride would be. The panel was pleasant to look at, as it was simply a large jet-black slate. I suppose you could call it a monolith. There was a basic map and some language that I couldn't possibly begin to understand. I assumed that the moving, blinking light on the map was the garden itself.

I left Cesca and the monolith, then wandered into the garden area to see that the girls were all sitting on a blanket. It seemed like a picnic was underway.

"We've got about an hour before we touch down." Yae passed a sandwich to me as I sat down between her and Yumina. It was just a standard ham and cheese, but I cocked my head in confusion after taking a bite.

"I-Is something wrong, is there?"

"No… nothing's wrong… It's just, uh, different from usual. It tastes better, actually."

"I-It does?!" Yae patted her own chest in relief. *Weird, though… it has more salt and pepper in it than Crea usually includes… Wait a second…*

"Yae… did you make this?"

"Y-Yes, I did… C-Crea-dono was teaching me, she was… I-I decided that i-if I was to be your wife, T-Touya-dono… then I should master the kitchen, a-alongside mastering the sword…"

*I see, that makes sense. Glad I didn't say anything careless, then…* I happily munched down on the sandwich, thanking Yae for her efforts.

"Here. I made this! You should try it."

"Hmm? You made something too, Elze? Sure, I'll give it a go."

"W-Wait, that's…" I reached out for the fried chicken that Elze had offered to me. Linze tried to mutter something, but it was too late. The fork was already in my mouth.

"Hh…"

"Well? Tasty, right?"

"Hhhhhhoht! Ugh! Sspischey! Mai thounghe! Hohthohthohthoht!!! Iht hurthts!" Yumina quickly passed me some water, but it wasn't nearly enough to help. Linze managed to produce a block of ice about the size of a basketball, so I rested my tongue on that. Crisis averted.

"I can't believe what you've given me… I can't believe it…" There were tears flowing down my face, but they sure as hell weren't tears of joy. *Just what was with that spicy chicken?!*

"Huh? Is it that hot?" Elze nonchalantly chowed down on the chicken, popping another piece into her mouth. While I was wondering how that brazen maniac was still breathing, Linze started to apologize on her behalf.

"My sister has a… freakish resistance to any kind of spice. When she cooks, she tends to make the hottest kinds of dishes imaginable… She wasn't permitted in the kitchen back at home for this reason." *Damn it, Linze, why didn't you speak up sooner? I didn't expect to feel this crippling sense of defeat before we even reached the Golem…*

At that moment, I resolved that Elze would never be allowed to cook in our household. It was simply too much of a health and safety hazard to let her near anything to do with cooking.

*Ugh… my tongue hurts so much… A-Are my lips swollen, too?!*

We arrived at the Melicia Mountain range and headed north. Before long, we came to a halt in the air directly above the Stael Mines. I peered down at the mining area directly below and opened up a [Gate] to drop us off at the surface. Cesca was left to hold down the fort on her own at the garden. From the moment we touched down, we noticed the whole area was wrapped in an almost eerie silence.

"Do you think everyone abandoned the area?"

"With a Golem roaming about, just about anyone'd do the same. Once those things take to an area, they tend to wipe out anyone or anything careless enough to get close. No need to go looking for it, I'm sure it'll come for us anyway." Yumina and Elze chatted a little while I ran a search on my map for "Mithril Golem." I found it pretty quickly. It was dead ahead, deep within the tunnels. In fact, it was heading in our direction.

"Okay, we should be good. Looks like the Golem's willing to bring the fight to us. I was worried about the possibility of a cave-in, but it looks like we'll be fine. Once it pops out, should I start throwing it around a bit with [Slip], maybe?"

"That wasss hell…"

"I could go without experiencing that ever again…" My idea seemed to have touched on a recent point of trauma for both Kokuyou and Sango.

"But will that work on a Golem? Unlike these two, a Golem won't beg you for forgiveness with tears in its eyes."

"You tryn'a ssstart sssomethin', fuzzball?"

"Kohaku… I would advise against that. We are not to be trifled with." I had to take a moment to calm those 3 down, or they'd have been at each other's throats for the rest of the day.

Still, Kohaku made a valid point. The actual physical damage I could deal with [Slip] wasn't that great, and I doubted I could beat a Golem relying on that alone. Even against Kokuyou and Sango, that strategy only worked because the fight was on a time limit.

*So, if I have to come up with something else… then there's something I've been wanting to try out.*

"I've gotta go grab a couple things. I'll be back in a sec." I left these words behind as I opened up a [Gate] to regroup with Cesca in the garden.

Upon finishing my preparations and returning to the mining area, I found that the Golem's footsteps had already come within earshot.

"Where the hell'd you run off to?! The damn thing's practically on top of us already!"

"Sorry, took longer to prepare than I thought." As I apologized to Elze, I ran over to Linze and Yumina and handed them each 50 rounds of [**Explosion**] bullets. I also gave my New Model Army to Yae along with a few bullets. She wouldn't be doing much in terms of firepower since her sword was useless, so you could never be too careful.

If things went as planned, then it shouldn't have to come to that anyway, but the best laid plans of mice and men often go awry, or so it went.

The Golem's thudding footsteps approached in tremors. It was about to take center stage any minute. I kept close watch on the tunnel entrance, only at that point noting how huge it was. I began to wonder if that tunnel had been dug by the Golem itself, rather than the miners. If so, then the Golem could well have been scraping its head along the ceiling of that trail.

The closer it grew, the stranger its footsteps sounded. It was almost as if there were two pairs of legs walking toward us…

"It's here, it is!" A giant silver body shot off reflections from the sunlight as it stepped out from within the darkness of the tunnel.

It was like a bunch of boulders all piled on top of each other, except for that brilliant metallic sheen to the whole thing. It had to be at least 6 meters tall. It stood on short legs and had large, long arms. Its face was blank and featureless, save for two small holes for eye sockets. Glowing, sickening red eyes glared at us from within.

"T-Touya, look!" Yumina pointed at the second Golem that steadily made its way out from the tunnel, just behind the first one. The second also shone silver in the sunlight.

*Two Mithril Golems? That's not what the information said! Guess this explains the second set of footsteps, though. Didn't even notice when I checked the map earlier... The two pins must've been overlapping each other at the time... They're sticking together like husband and wife! If I'd only zoomed in on them at the time, I'd have known beforehand that we'd have to deal with a pair of them... Hell, at this point, I wouldn't be surprised if a little tiny Golem kid came running out from behind them.*

While I stood there thinking stupid things, one of the Golems had picked up a great big boulder and launched it at us. *Damn it, watch out!* We all split up and dodged the incoming boulder. It crashed into the ground with great force, shattering to pieces and sending rubble in all directions.

**"Come forth, Water! Ballistic Bubbles: [Bubble Bomb]!"** Linze let loose a small cloud of bubbles and steered them in the Golem's direction. The moment the first one made contact, it started a chain of explosions that roared deafeningly throughout the area.

A mist-like smokescreen was the only evidence the attack had ever happened. The Golem itself wasn't so much as scratched.

"No effect whatsoever...?" Elemental compatibility probably had a lot to do with that. I vaguely remembered hearing that Earth-elementals had strong resistances against Water-type magic.

Yumina and Yae shot at the Golem repeatedly. Each of the bullets exploded upon impact, but it still didn't so much as put a dent in the Golem's defenses.

If we kept fighting like that, we had slim chances of victory. And so, I decided to put my plan into motion.

"I've got a plan. Everyone, fall back!" Nobody seemed to get what I was talking about at first, but they fell back like I asked all the same. The Golem rushed straight for me. Perhaps because it was a Mithril Golem, it moved a lot faster than I'd normally have expected one to be able to. Still, light as it was for something of its size, it was still a huge lump of metal.

*If this doesn't work, I'll just have to come up with something fast.*

"[Accel]!" I activated my acceleration spell and dived straight beneath the beast's lurched chest. As soon as I found myself within range, I slapped my palm against the ground and chanted the spell that formed the core of my plan.

"[Gate]!" Both Golems, their onslaught now thwarted by the huge hole opened beneath their feet, sank through what used to be ground as though it had suddenly turned to water. My plan had worked.

"T-Touya, did you just...?"

"Yeah, I blasted them off with [Gate]." Yumina asked, and I confirmed her suspicions. Honestly, I was just glad it had all worked.

"So, where did you send them, then?" In response to Yae's question, I grinned and pointed straight upward.

"Straight up. Ten thousand meters into the sky."

"What?!" I left the girls to recover from their state of complete confusion, then confirmed the locations of both Golems on my map. It didn't display how high they were, but two pins did show up on the map, a little off from where we were standing. Considering air resistance and momentum and whatnot, it made sense that they wouldn't just fall down in a straight line. In this case, though, I was glad for the distance between us, since the last thing we needed was a pair of Mithril Golems dropping straight down on our heads. There was a mining town to the south of where we were, but the Golems weren't falling in that direction, so that was fine.

I had returned to the garden to ask Cesca to raise its altitude to ten-thousand meters for exactly this purpose. Though, looking back, that may have been fairly overkill.

I only remembered the existence of terminal velocity after I'd already dropped the Golems. *Because a falling object faces strong air resistance, it can only accelerate up to a certain speed and then maintain that. At that point, the fall distance stops mattering. Everything past that point is unnecessary... I'll just brush this little blunder aside as me making doubly sure that it worked properly.*

With a shrill metallic screech and a thunderous boom, the two hunks of metal came crashing to the ground slightly west of where we were. I was a little bit surprised by where they had landed. I hadn't expected them to drop straight down in front of us, but they'd landed further away than I'd thought.

I activated [**Accel**] and rushed over to where they'd fallen. Everyone else also activated the [**Accel**] in their rings and kept up with my pace.

"Damn, they're *still* moving?" Both Golems, now covered in dents and cracks, forced themselves to their feet inside their small craters. That had dealt a lot less damage than I'd thought. Was mithril really such a light metal? The Golems resumed their rushing assault on us.

"**Come forth, Water! Ballistic Bubbles: [Bubble Bomb]**" Linze cast a spell to halt their advance, and this time, the shockwave from the blasts sent chunks of metal flying off from the cracked body of the one in front. It was a lot more effective now. I caught sight of a dull silver ball hidden within the chest of the first Golem. That was probably its core.

**"[Accel Boost]!"** Elze coupled her own physical strengthening magic with the acceleration spell in her ring and shot toward the Golem like a speeding bullet. Her gauntlet let out a red flash as she crashed her fully-charged punch into the enemy.

The horrible sound of metal colliding with metal rang out as a chunk of the Golem's core was blasted off. The Golem fell lifeless to the ground, the force of its huge frame crashing down sending small tremors through the ground.

Turning my attention to the other Golem, I caught sight of Yae firing several explosive bullets at it with the New Model Army gun that I'd handed her. The sounds of gunfire and explosions rang out in rapid succession.

This other Golem's chest was also blasted apart from the force of the explosions, just like with the first one. In another similarity to the other, its core came into plain sight.

**"Strike true, Lightning! Hundredspear Thunderclap: [Lightning Javelin]!"** Seeing her chance, Yumina unleashed a number of lightning blasts straight at the Golem's exposed core. The core was split in half with a sharp shattering noise. Its power source destroyed, the second Golem also fell limply onto its back.

Both Golems had ceased moving, and the area had become littered with dust clouds and shattered chunks of mithril. Once the fight was over, I realized that I hadn't done anything at all to help at the end there…

"A job well done."

"All I really did was open up a **[Gate],** that's all…" I couldn't help but return Kohaku's praise with a forced smile.

Elze took the shattered core from the first Golem, and Yae retrieved the split core of the second. Each core was roughly the size of a volleyball, and they were a much duller silver than the rest of the Golem's body.

"We got the proof that we beat them, so that's this quest taken care of." Elze held up one of the cores with a bright smile. Right, we'd taken care of the quest. It was the cleanup I had been dreading. Putting their main bodies aside, it would take all day to go and pick up all the shattered chunks of mithril that had been sent flying all over the place... Unless I could use **[Storage]** to sift the mithril out from amongst all the regular rocks. It was worth a short.

"**[Storage]: In╱mithril.**" A magic circle spread out beneath my feet, and the Golem on the ground was perfectly absorbed by my storage spell. I investigated the ground around where it had collapsed, and not a pebble of mithril was left on the ground. Another lucky break.

I went over and stored the second Golem's body away, too. The capacity of **[Storage]** was largely influenced by the magic of the user, meaning that most people wouldn't have been able to store a whole Golem away like I was able to do.

"Alright, let's head home for the day." *We can just report in to the guild tomorrow. We've already retrieved both Golems, cores and all, so there's no need to rush.*

I opened up a **[Gate]** to the mansion's back garden, and we were immediately greeted by the sight of Renne practicing on a bicycle and Cecile watching over her. Renne was wearing a shirt and trousers with suspenders instead of her usual maid outfit. She was sporting a more boyish look, and from all the dirt she was covered in, I could only assume she'd been practicing hard on that bike. *Today was Renne's day off, so Cecile must be watching over her in between her own work.*

"Welcome baaack, sir."

"Hey there, Cecile." Renne heard Cecile call out to us, so she spun her bike around and shot straight at us. Then, she hit the breaks and skidded to a halt in front of us. Evidently, she had mastered the vehicle already. And faster than the duke had, at that. Seemed kids really were fast learners.

"Welcome back, bruv!"

"Looks like you've already mastered the bike, eh, Renne?"

"Aye!" She shot me such a beaming smile that I couldn't resist patting her on the head. Times like that, seeing Renne having so much fun with that bike, made me really glad I'd decided to build one.

*For now, we should go have a bath and wash off all this dust and dirt. Renne can go in with the other girls. I'll just use the bath when they're done.*

"Huh?" We turned to walk into the mansion when Renne shot us a puzzled look. Was there something the matter?

"Where's Cesca at?"

"… Whoops." Five delayed reactions came to us in perfect harmony.

*… Aww, crap. I completely forgot.*

"No, I do not mind it. Indeed, I do not care about being left behind, Master. Not at all. Truly — *not one bit.*"

*Cesca's smile is scaring me… Usually, she's not one to show much emotion, so why the hell does she only smile at times like this…?*

"Thanks to this experience, I've learned that you have a fetish for leaving girls by themselves. Sooner or later, this perversion of yours will have you forcing me to get naked and stay in the park all by myself at night. You will enjoy yourself as I quiver with fear at the idea of being seen or assaulted. Truly, your tastes are highly refined, Master."

"None of that *ever* crossed my mind!"

*She's just mad about being left behind! Well, yeah, it's our fault and all, but it's become a habit of mine to open a* [**Gate**] *and go back whenever we're done hunting.*

"Just leave it at that. He clearly feels guilty about it, and if you push it too far, he might actually leave you, you know?" Leen was sitting in the garden, sipping at the black tea Cesca had prepared for her.

"Hmph. That would be quite troublesome. Therefore, Master, I will forgive you if you present me with a set of lewd underwear that suits your tastes."

"Aren't you asking for a bit *too* much?! I couldn't do that even if the underwear *wasn't* lewd!"

"It was a joke." Cesca bowed her head and exited the terrace.

*If only there was someone who could do something about that robot girl's inner workings.* Leen looked at Cesca as she continued walking away.

"I have to say, I'm impressed. By her mental abilities, I mean."

"What the hell is so impressive about that perverted mind of hers?!"

"Oh, I'm not referring to her personality. It's more about the way she expresses her irritation or the flexibility that allows her to crack jokes. She's almost like a real human. I'm not sure if it's possible to create something like her with [**Program**]…"

*Hey, you shouldn't say that. That little stuffed bear in the corner of the terrace is getting visibly upset. I'm actually pretty impressed by*

*the way it's kicking that pebble with its arms behind its back… It's a*
*worthy match to Cesca, really.*

"So, what brought you here today?"

"Well, it was about the remaining Babylon teleportation circles…
I haven't located any concrete information so far."

"Hm? You're thinking of searching for them?"

"Hmm? You're *not,* then?" We were both caught in surprise.
Honestly, I wasn't too enthusiastic about the idea. Cesca alone was
too much to handle, and I had no idea how it would get if I got even
more… The doctor herself said that she didn't care whether I did or
didn't find them.

"I can't really think of a reason to search for them…"

"Why?! Don't you want to discover more ancient knowledge or
lost technology?!"

"Nope."

"Ghh, what a dreamless youngster you are!" Well, true, I *was*
a youngster compared to her. But the doctor said that the power of
Babylon wouldn't be needed in this era.

That being said, we did have to consider the Phrase. If we
wanted to be on the safe side, it might've been a good idea to take
everything Babylon had to offer.

Even so, if we couldn't find the teleportation circles, there was
nothing for us to do.

"Let's think of what to do when we get some new information. If
you manage to locate a teleportation circle, I'll be there to help you
out."

"…Make it a promise. If you don't keep it, I'll have you buy lewd
underwear for me, too."

"Please, anything but that!" I pushed my forehead against the
table and begged. If I bought lewd underwear for someone as young-

looking as her, my life would be over in an entirely different way. Hell, I didn't even know if such underwear existed. Satisfied with my promise, Leen and Paula returned to the royal palace. *I hope this doesn't become too troublesome…*

"Two Mithril Golems… Forgive us. There was an error in our investigation." The guild's receptionist bowed her head. There was no error in the fact that it was a Golem hunting quest, but since the goal was to liberate the mines, it should've specified that we had to defeat *two* Golems.

"In cases like this, you are paid for both of the monsters and, to make up for the failure on our part, we double the reward, meaning that you get ten platinum coins. The points for your guild card are doubled, too, of course."

*Well, isn't that nice. Though, I guess it's only fair to do this.*

She placed ten platinum coins on the counter and pushed the stamp onto our cards.

"The points you just received have raised your guild rank. Congratulations." We took our cards back. Yumina's was blue, while the rest were red.

*With this, we're now first class adventurers. Oh? There's something next to the Dragon Slayer symbol. It's square and seems to display a silhouette reminiscent of a cracked Golem's head.*

"Also, for completing this quest, the guild presents you with the proof that you defeated a Golem — the title of Golem Buster." *I see. So it's a new symbol, huh?* The privilege granted by the Golem Buster title was a 20% off in all shops sponsored by the guild, but the Dragon Slayer title already gave us 30% off, so it didn't mean much.

Once we left the guild, Linze and Yumina went to the magic shop, while Elze went to train with General Leon. I had Kohaku go with Linze and Yumina, while Sango and Kokuyou joined Elze. That setup allowed me to stay in touch with them in case something happened. A part of me expected the telepathy between me and my summons to stop working at greater distances, but apparently it didn't really matter. *There's something wrong with using them as a replacement for phones, though.*

Yae and I made plans to go to a blacksmith. I thought of using the mithril we got to forge Yae a new sword, but no normal smiths in the area could work with katanas. *I guess the only place for katana-related business is Eashen.*

I opened a [Gate] and walked out into Oedo. Normally, this would've been the time to go to Yae's parents and ask for her hand, but since I only just met them last time I visited, I was a bit reluctant to go through with it. It wasn't like the marriage was happening anytime soon, so it was best to save it for later. Yae herself agreed, so I just left it at that.

Apparently, there was a really good katana smith in the western edge of Oedo, opposite to where Yae's home was. As the two of us made our way there, I couldn't help but notice how Yae would occasionally glance at me.

"Hm? Something wrong?"

"Uhh?! Ah, n-nothing, just that… Touya-dono and I are now arranged to be married… correct?"

"Huh? Y-Yeah. That's right." The way she said that made it seem like we were promised to each other by our parents, but the meaning was the same. Honestly, it made me a bit shy.

"I-If that is so, then… W-Well… m-m-may we h-hold hands as we walk, m-may we…?" Red to her ears, she spoke those words while slightly looking down.

*What the hell?! That's really damn cute! Is there a single guy in the world who could say no to that?! Nay, I say! And I'm no different!*

I slowly extended my right hand and grabbed her left.

Ah… Her hand was as soft as it was back when I used [**Recall**].

She looked up to me, smiled in an oh-so-adorable manner, and gripped my hand tight. Actions like that always made my heart skip a beat.

I had no idea that walking hand-in-hand with a girl I liked was such bliss… I could totally understand why couples throughout all worlds just couldn't stop flirting. *Let it be known that there is no sin in this.*

We approached the smithy at the western edge of Oedo, ended our short date, and walked into the very noisy shop.

"Hello? Is anyone here?"

"Yes. You need something?" A woman in her early twenties walked out to greet us. Her black hair was tied back behind her and she was wearing a pair of sandals… *I think she's an employee?*

"I need someone to forge a katana. Is this the right place?"

"A katana? Yes, you're right where you need to be. Wait just a moment. Sweetheart! You have a customer!" She called out to the forge, which was deeper inside the building. *Oh, so she's the missus.*

A thirty-or-so year old man came out to see us. He was clad in monk-like work clothes and wearing a towel on his head like a bandana. He had a manly beard, but it did nothing to detract from the fact that he had a very gentle face. *He looks like a friendly mountain man… Not a good comparison, but still.*

"A katana, eh? For which one of ya?"

"Ah, for her. I'd like to have it made from mithril…"

"Mithril?! Now ain't that fancy! You the son of some lord or somethin'?" The smith couldn't hide his surprise. His wife was no different in that regard.

"Nah, we got it from a Mithril Golem we defeated. I decided to make good use of it and make her a weapon."

"Ah, I see. To down a Mithril Golem… You two are stronger than you look, ain't ya?" The smith sighed, but he looked decidedly impressed. He then asked to see Yae's katana and short sword. After taking it in hand, examining and correcting it while squinting his eyes, he gave us a date.

"It'll be done in a week. That alright with ya?"

"Sounds great. Thanks a lot. So, how much will that be?"

"Cash ain't necessary."

*Eh? Pardon? Is he saying it's for free? When you consider the saying 'there's no such thing as free lunch'… it makes me think there'll be a catch. Some things sound too good to be true and all beautiful roses have thorns… Nothing is more expensive than something that's free, as my grandma used to say.*

"I don't need money, but could you spare me some of your mithril, instead? Eashen does have hihi'irokane, but mithril is nearly impossible to get. And bringing it over from the west costs an arm and a leg, you know?" *Ah, so that's how it is.*

"I'm okay with that, but I have no clue how much it's worth, so I have no idea how much I should leave with you."

"I see… For now, just leave enough for me to make the katana and short sword. When I'm done, you'll pay with as much mithril as you think the work deserves."

"We'll go with that, then. Have a good day, now!" *I'll have to research mithril's market value before the week ends.* I opened my **[Storage]** and took out a chunk of mithril about the size of a softball.

"Is this enough?"

"Yep. Bit too much, actually." He took the mithril in hand and shook it up and down, as if to measure its weight.

"See you next week, then!"

"Thank you very much for your patronage!" The blacksmith's wife waved us goodbye as we took our leave.

When we arrived at a place with no people, I tried to open a [Gate], but Yae took hold of the hem of my coat and hesitantly looked up at me.

"U-Umm… c-can it be just the t-two of us… a while longer, can it…?" Her face turned red as her head drooped low.

*Damn it! If we weren't in town, I'd hug her right here and now!* I took Yae's hand in mine, which made her let out a shy smile, and began walking the streets of Oedo with her.

"What is that, sir?" Lapis inquired about the nature of "that," which I had made through use of [Modeling].

On the object, three blades formed a propeller fan contained within a protective cage. The fan was attached to a pole that connected to a round base.

It was a staple of the summer season, the great electric fan. I was disappointed that I hadn't been able to make one out of plastic, but mithril did the job well enough due to how light it was.

"Begin [Program]／Starting Condition: A switch on the fan is pressed／Upon Switch Pressed: Spin the fan with the force appropriate to the switch／End [Program]." I pressed the "Weak" switch on the fan, and it came steadily to life. The fan rotated gently, sending cool air throughout the room.

"A device for controlling wind, is it? Amazing!"

"Hrmm…" In contrast to Lapis' amazement, I felt kind of let down.

Originally, I had wanted to build a car, but assembling the engine had proved to be way more than I could handle. Having an example of the object I wanted to build sitting in front of me was one thing, but I couldn't even fathom what purpose half the parts served just from photographs and blueprints alone.

I understood the basic principles by which car engines worked, but there were too many fiddly bits that I just couldn't wrap my head around. It all just made my head hurt. I wasn't even very good with machines in the first place. I'd always been more of a bookworm type, actually. That was why I gave up pretty quickly.

When I realized that I wouldn't have any fuel even if I *did* somehow create a functioning engine, my thoughts briefly switched to building a steam engine instead, but that was another idea that I quickly scrapped.

The next thing to come to mind was a motor. A motor wasn't nearly as complex as a car engine, and I felt that I could probably build one. That was when it hit me. I could very likely just use [**Program**] to achieve the exact same effect.

To test the idea, I assembled an electric fan without any of the electric parts, then slapped a simple [**Program**] onto it. That test was currently cooling the room quite successfully. I couldn't help but feel that [**Program**] was way too overpowered when it came to this stuff.

Was science utterly powerless before the all-encompassing might of magic? This wasn't something that just anyone could make, but it *was* something that anybody with any amount of magic could use. There were no problems in that regard, but… for some reason, the whole thing had left me feeling kind of listless.

It was true that even [**Program**] probably wasn't strong enough to turn a big box on wheels into a functioning car. Not *alone,* at least. With the right enchantments, I could probably have pulled it off. It would be like an oversized toy car, though, with no engine noise, no vibration from the motor, no real contents whatsoever.

The thought drained away all of my motivation, which was why I gave up after building a non-electric fan. It wasn't like we were in desperate need of a car, anyhow.

I gave the fan to Lapis and told her to use it as she saw fit. It should've at least kept working as long as people fed tiny bits of magic into it every now and then. I looked up at the roof and thought in passing about how a ceiling fan might be a nice addition to the room.

"Shall we get going, Touya?" Yumina came up to me as I walked out into the garden from the terrace. Was it that time already?

We were about to depart to meet the king and queen of Belfast, so that I could tell them that I intended to marry their daughter. Technically, we had already been engaged this whole time, but I thought it best to let them know I was serious about it now.

*To think that Yumina would win me over in less than a year... Didn't think I'd fold so quickly, but I've got no regrets.*

"Look, I know I said I'm serious about marrying you and everything now, but... Are they gonna force me to be king at this rate?"

"Hmm... That seems the most likely outcome, yes. It might turn out different if father or uncle have a son, however."

"What about if Sue took a husband... Couldn't you just make him king instead?" That was about the only other thing I could think of. Taking the throne as king after marrying into royal blood seemed perfectly reasonable. Though really, I'd feel kind of sorry about just forcing all that responsibility on them in my place.

"That certainly would be one option, if not for one simple fact."

"What's that, then?"

"Well, Sue loves you too, after all. I'd say she's the most likely to become the fifth."

"...The fifth?"

She said it so casually that it made me pause for a moment. *The fifth... No, that can't be right. That can't be what she's talking about, right?*

"Well, it doesn't seem like that will be anytime soon, at any rate. But, say maybe three, four years down the line? She'll probably approach you about it, so you should brace yourself for that while you can."

"Nah, I think you're just overthinking it. Sue doesn't have any siblings, right? I'm sure she just sees me as an older brother or something."

"...It seems I'll need to prepare myself for a lot of *this,* too..." Yumina sighed, apparently having given up on some fundamental aspect of my personality. *What? What's the issue here?*

"The only other way to find someone else to take the throne would be if we, you know, had a son together, or something..." Yumina trailed off. She kept staring at me, which only made her blush with greater intensity.

*Damn it, now you're making me turn bright red, too! It's because you started talking about us having kids all of a sudden!*

"Sh-Shall we proceed?"

"Y-Yes. We shall." Barely even holding a conversation anymore, we walked out into the garden, and I opened up a **[Gate]** to take us to the castle.

"I see! Well, that's wonderful news! I'm glad to hear that Yumina's won over your heart. How truly joyous indeed!" The king of Belfast leaned forward and shot me a great, big, happy smile. Queen Yuel took her daughter's hands in her own and smiled gently at her.

"You've done well for yourself, Yumina. From now on, you only need to worry about how best to support Touya as his wife."

"Yes, Mother!" The king rose from his chair and gave me a jolly old pat on the shoulder. He was really over the moon with this news.

"All I need to wait for now is the day I get to see my grandchildren! I imagine it'll be hard satisfying four wives, but you do your best, you hear me?"

*Do my best at what? Do you even realize what you're saying, Your Majesty?*

"Look, I'm saying I *intend* to marry her, not that we're getting married *right away*. All of that's on hold until I turn eighteen, at the very least."

"Even if the wedding's still a while off, it's not like that's stopping you from making me some grandkids! After all, Yumina's already started her— Mhrf?!" Yumina's fist smashed magnificently into the king's solar plexus, making him double over. She *definitely* just used [**Accel**] against him…

"Father, you don't just casually mention things like that!" Yumina was bright red and exhaling heavily. Groveling at her feet, his face pale and writhing in pain, was His Royal Majesty the King of Belfast, the most important man in the country. *You reap what you sow. Even if she is your own daughter, that was pretty much sexual harassment. Definitely shouldn't be saying those kinds of things out loud.*

"I'm sorry about my husband. He's just so excited to hear the news, you see." Queen Yuel apologized in her husband's place. It wasn't a bad thing to be excited, I just felt that he was getting excited about all the wrong things.

"Now really, how should we handle this… There are plenty who know of the situation already, but it might still be a bit soon to announce this to the public."

"How come?"

"First of all, you'd definitely be targeted by nobles who had thought to marry into the royal family. On the other end of the scale, you have those who would try to win your favor early for political reasons or the like. In addition to that, there are those stubborn few who would stand firmly against the whole thing unless you showed suitable accomplishments in the name of the country." None of what she said sounded fun in the least. It all just served to remind me how marrying a princess was kind of a big deal.

*Accomplishments in the name of the country? Basically, they'd want me to prove that I'd be a beneficial asset to the country before they'd approve of me?*

"Let's keep word of this to ourselves for a while longer. Announcing it too early would lead to a lot of unwanted trouble, so it may be best to keep it a secret for as long as possible and then announce your betrothal just shortly before the wedding itself." *Seems like I'll have to do my best as well if I want to live up to all of this... I'll become a worthy partner for Yumina.*

I left Yumina with her parents and headed in the direction of the training grounds. I was hoping to catch Elze there, but it seemed my hope was in vain. She was nowhere to be found. The sounds of mock battles spread out across the training ground. It was honestly pretty exciting to watch. Sort of reminded me of the feeling of watching a sports match. There were a lot of knights out training, as well.

"You there, cur. What are *you* doing here?" I turned to face the voice, and found myself looking at a group of young men. There seemed to be about ten of them. They didn't look too far from my age. Well, maybe one or two of them were a little older. I couldn't say for sure, really. I wondered if they were knights, too.

"Yes, mongrel, I meant you. I don't recognize your face. Which house are you the servant of? You know this training ground is an *exclusive* area, don't you? You should really take more care where you wander."

"Oh, no. It's nothing like that. I'm just looking around for a friend of mine. I thought she was here."

A young man standing at the head of the group, one with short golden-blond hair, spoke up. He spoke in a haughty, arrogant tone of voice, as if he was looking down on me for whatever reason. It seemed to me that he had the wrong impression. I figured the best thing to do would be to correct him and move on.

"And which friend might this be?"

"Oh, do you think he's referring to that lowborn woman? The one who accompanies General Leon so often these days." A redheaded boy in the back answered the blondie's question. That sounded about right. Elze did prefer to spar with Leon after all.

"Oh. *That* girl… Haaa… trying to curry favor with the general, are we? Truly those of lower birth have no integrity at all, pathetic…" The one to speak up this time was a brown-haired boy standing next to Redhead. He had a smug grin plastered on his face.

"I see. This one must be trying to join the army too. He's using that girl as a foot in the door."

"This military won't get anywhere unless someone sets it straight. Frankly, it'd be better if we didn't allow commoners to serve at all. They have no sense of chivalry, unlike us proud sons of the noble houses." The group of boy-knights threw their heads back in raucous laughter. I turned on my heel to leave, as they were seriously annoying me.

"Actually… could it be that the girl is your woman?"

"And what if she is?" I paused to answer the brown-haired teen, who decided to yell after me. His shrill laughter was driving me mad with irritation.

"In that case, if you're looking for her, why not look in the general's bed? I'm sure she's there right about now, moaning like the lowborn dog she is!"

I didn't let him continue his budding tirade. Before Brown-hair knew it, my fist was in his face. He fell to the ground, clutching at himself. Blood pooled from his nose, and a few of his teeth were scattered across the floor. I turned and kicked him hard in the side, just for good measure.

"Ghaugh! Whhuh... what are you doing?!"

"I'm clearly beating the hell out of you. What, do you need me to spell it out?" Brown-hair was on the floor, rolling in pain as he clutched his side. He still managed to yell at me, though. I kicked him again. Harder.

If he had just mocked me, I'd have been able to let it go. But I wasn't the kind of person who could stand around and let the people precious to him be slandered. It was like my grandpa always said. If you need to beat on someone, then beat them savagely without hesitation.

"You scum! That's the second son of the distinguished Barrow family! You dare lay a hand on—"

"Shut it. You're making a racket. Why does his family matter right now? It's not like he, or you for that matter, have anything great about you as individuals. You're just lazy little shits who rest on the laurels of their family crests, right?"

"How dare you!" The young knights quickly surrounded me in a circle. They all pulled out their blades. I could tell they weren't messing around. They were clearly set on harming, if not killing, me.

"So you've drawn your swords on me. You understand what that means, right? The only ones who should aim to kill are those who are prepared to be killed."

"Silence, commoner!" One of the boys charged at me with a slash, but his form was poor. *Geez, that's almost embarrassingly bad. Have any of these guys done any actual training?*

"Safety Mode." In accordance to my words, Brunhild extended into a longsword with a dulled, rounded blade. *Nothing sharp at all on this bad boy.* This was a new form I'd added to my weapon, for safety purposes. Well… maybe safety wasn't quite the right term for it. If I decided to swing it at full power it could definitely crush someone's bones. Anyway, I charged at another incoming swordsman, wielding Brunhild.

"Gah!" The boy stumbled and collapsed to the ground. *Too many openings, punk. I could beat you blindfolded.*

The "knights" watched as their friend was knocked down, and began to hesitate in their movements. *Pathetic.*

"Everyone charge in at once! Slash him at the same time!" Blondie barked out an order. Guess that made him their leader. Still, was he a total moron? What kind of chump *yelled out his strategy* before using it?

I decided to attack them before they made their move. Their attacks were so telegraphed that dodging was trivial. I was easily able to strike three of them in the belly, the chest, and the arm. They went down like a sack of bricks.

The others saw my motion and began to seize up in fear. They were absurdly miserable people.

I swung my weapon without putting too much effort into it, and before long they were all down for the count. All except Blondie. The last man standing.

"E-Eek! Auuuugh!!!" Blondie started screaming like a little girl, turned tail, and ran away as fast as he could. *Some chivalry and honor you've got there. Really shows when you abandon your allies and turn your back on the enemy.*

"Gun Mode." I returned Brunhild to its gun form, then fired off a bullet. Pow.

"Gwuhh?!" I couldn't be bothered to chase after him, so I just fired a paralyzing round into his back. Blondie fell to the floor with a crash, then stopped moving entirely. *Guess that's that... Now, where was I?*

"Eek!" The only one still conscious was Brown-hair, lying down in a pool of his own fluids. I couldn't possibly forgive him for saying what he did about Elze.

"Could you leave it at that, please?" I looked up for the source of the sudden voice, and caught sight of two older knights standing nearby. I recognized one of them, but the other was an older gentleman with silvery hair. He looked about forty.

"Lyon...!"

"What's up, Sir Touya. Long time no see." The handsome young gent raised his hand to me in a wave. It was Lyon, the good knight that had accompanied us to Mismede. General Leon's son.

"D-Deputy General, sir! Th-This lout came out of nowhere, a-and he... he...!" Brown-hair pointed at me, seemingly addressing the silver-haired man next to Lyon. *Deputy general?*

"...Boy. Do you think my eyes blind to the trouble you and your friends cause for the townspeople? You think my ears deaf to the concern regarding your names?" The silver-haired man let out a deep voice, devoid of emotion. He was staring directly at the brown-haired kid. In response, the boy stiffened up in fear and fell silent. It seemed this kind of attitude wasn't a new thing for them. So they definitely were the kind of people who thought they could do whatever they wanted... I found that kind of person very irritating.

"I understand that your family has been covering for you using their name, but that won't save you anymore. Now I see you all attack one man in a group, but lose regardless of your cheap tactics. And your little 'leader' ran away like an animal upon seeing his friends defeated. Disgusting. Not a single one of you are fit to be called knights." Lyon spoke with a surprising intensity behind his words. I could tell he felt a lot of shame that these boys were calling themselves Belfastian Knights.

"You'll soon be informed of your penalties and expulsions. Tell your unconscious friends that, as well. And before you get any funny ideas, don't go thinking about revenge. If you lay a single hand on this man, your noble families will incur high levels of disgrace. That, I promise you." The deputy general turned his attention away from Brown-hair and looked at me. Once our eyes met, he bowed his head.

"I'm truly sorry for these wretches. Please know that their behavior is not something that represents the Belfastian Knights."

"...Nah, don't worry about that. I went a little overboard, too." *Calm down, Touya. You've really done it this time... You definitely didn't need to knock those guys out with your sword! There were plenty of other ways you could've incapacitated them, right? Gah! It's not my fault... When that asshole spoke badly of Elze I just saw red... I definitely need more training or something.*

"Ah, you're much too kind... I'm the deputy general of the Belfastian knight order, Neil Suleiman."

"Mochizuki Touya. Nice to meet you."

"Oh I'm well aware of who you are, young man. You're quite the celebrity in my social circles." I had... mixed feelings about that, but I still shook the man's hand with a smile on my face.

After I apologized to Deputy General Neil, Lyon spoke up about the current state of the knight order.

It seemed that the knights took charge of protecting the capital, guarding the citizens of the kingdom, guarding the royal family, and escorting important individuals. Most were sons from noble families, but usually second or third-born, the oldest sons were the successors, and therefore too important to risk in the line of duty. Apparently those sons only enlisted to boast about their family and social class, rather than out of any sense of duty.

"I'm the second son of my household, actually. But unlike other noble families, we'd get the crap pounded out of us if we did anything bad like those punks…" Lyon wore a wry smile on his face as he spoke. *Well, you do have Leon for a father…* Lyon certainly didn't seem spoiled at all to me, which was probably a good thing. Neil also explained that he was the second son of a rather affluent count.

"They're a minority, it's true, but unfortunately there are those who cling to their heritage like it's all they have. A recruit from an earl's house might refuse to listen to their viscount-born commander, or a captain might try to suck up to a newbie just because he's from a better social background. It's a complete farce, if you ask me." Neil's expression was one of pure, unbridled disgust. Seemed like there were always troublemakers, no matter where you looked.

"Well, it's definitely curtains for this lot. They're pathetic parasites on our proud order! Until now they've managed to avoid it through their family connections, but that won't fly this time. They attacked the man engaged to this country's princess, after all… They should consider themselves lucky their heads are still attached to their necks." He must've been watching from the start. I'd be willing to bet he let it play out just so he could punish them for it… Well, I beat them up anyway, so it was no big deal.

"That aside… That weapon at your hip, what is it exactly?" Neil pointed a curious gaze toward Brunhild, my gunblade.

"Oh, this thing? It's my personal weapon. Only I can wield it, and only I can create it. I can use it for close combat or to take out targets from afar. Depending on its mode, it can become either a shortsword or a longsword, and it can fire paralyzing shots as well."

"Hmhm… It's a wonderful weapon indeed. Could I bother you to make one for me? Naturally, I'd pay you top coin for it."

"Sorry, but I don't think that's such a good idea…" I definitely had to be careful with regards to firearms. They were things that could kill people very easily. I'd have to be careful to only give them to people I had absolute confidence in.

"I see… What a shame."

"Oh, I could make you another kind of transforming weapon or a paralyzing weapon, though! If you can handle it, that is…"

"Seriously?! I'd absolutely love one!" By the time Neil had finished speaking, I had already cast [**Storage**] and pulled out an iron ingot. Mithril was sturdy, but it was far too lightweight to forge a regular weapon out of. Much too light to be effective. In fact, its lightness really only made it suitable for a thrusting-based sword like an estoc, or a sword primarily designed for slashing attacks.

"So, Neil, what kind of weapon do you prefer to use?"

"Well, my signature is definitely the spear, but I'm fine with a standard blade, too." *Hmm… that makes two forms, but maybe I should add in a dagger mode too, just for good measure.*

I used [**Modeling**] to craft a spear that was about two meters long. I based it on a western-style spear I'd seen in a video game before, but I changed the blade tip to be more dagger-like. To be blunt, it was more like a dagger with a really long handle.

I designed the grip itself to be hollow, allowing it to shift mass by filling the interior as it shortened in its transformation to dagger mode.

Similar to Brunhild, the thick dagger blade could thin out, which would allow it to extend itself into a one-meter longsword…

probably. I enchanted the sword with [**Modeling**]. And voila! It was complete.

"**Begin [Program]╱Starting Condition: The wielder says 'Spear Mode,' 'Sword Mode,' or 'Dagger Mode'╱Action Upon Start: [Modeling] casts upon the weapon, transforming it into the user-specified form╱End [Program].**" *Oh, almost forgot to give it the paralyzing effect.* I hastily enchanted the new product with [**Paralyze**].

"**Begin [Program]╱Starting Condition: The wielder says 'Stun Mode'╱Action Upon Start: Dull the blade of the weapon, and use the [Paralyze] spell to imbue it with the ability to stun anyone the blade touches╱End [Program].**"

"Uhh, I guess that's about it." I tried to spin the spear around. But, much like the one from back in Eashen, the balance on it was pretty terrible. I was probably just out of practice.

"Dagger Mode." The grip suddenly shunted and got shorter, making way for a dagger blade about 40 centimeters in length. I gave it a few test swings, and it responded quite nicely. I had a feeling that this form would be the easiest one to keep it in when carrying it around.

"Sword Mode." The blade expanded this time, becoming a meter-long shortsword. The handle also extended, allowing it to be gripped by both hands if necessary. I held it in front of me and gave it a test swing. *Yup, not bad at all.*

"Spear Mode." It returned to its initial state with no issues. *Okay, the transformation works well enough… Now to test the other part…*

"Stun Mode."

"Huh?" I had a ridiculously annoying grin on my face as I tapped Lyon on the shoulder with the spear tip. In but a moment, he crumpled like a puppet with its strings cut.

"Hahaugh?!"

"Yup, the paralysis seems to work just fine."

"Hey now..." Neil spoke up. He sounded a little mad, honestly. *What? I had to test it, didn't I?* Stun mode dulled the blade, so there was no harm done. Well... thrusting the spear would probably still hurt. I had set the paralysis to a weak effect, too, but it would still be about an hour before Lyon was able to get back up. I didn't want to wait that long, so I dispelled it with **[Recovery].**

"Hey, what was that for?!"

"Sorry, had to be sure it all worked right." I apologized to the complaining Lyon as I returned the weapon to blade mode and handed it over to Neil.

"It's hand-crafted, so the balance isn't especially good, but I think it should handle just fine after you get used to it." Neil took the spear from me, spun it around, thrust it forward, and did a sweeping strike. His motions were both clean and swift. Guess I shouldn't have expected anything else from a deputy general.

He cycled through the different transformations, performing similar clean motions with the dagger and sword forms. He then transformed it back into spear mode and pointed the tip toward Lyon.

"Stun Mode."

"Whoa, whoa, hold on a minute!"

"Heh, I'm just messing around." Neil gave a short chuckle and returned his weapon to its dagger form. Seemed he had no problem getting the hang of it.

"The paralysis effect in stun mode won't do anything to an enemy with a protective charm on them, so keep that in mind. Oh, and be careful where you swing it. Anyone affected won't be getting up for about an hour at least, so it'd be troublesome if you hit one of your allies."

"Very well, then. Thank you." Neil gazed at his dagger, seeming quite happy all the while. I was glad to have been of service.

"You sure are lucky to have such a thing, Deputy General."

"Hm? I can make one for you too, Lyon. If you'd like one, I mean."

"Really, Sir Touya?! You really mean it?!" I quickly whipped up another weapon of similar design and passed it over to Lyon. He started to cycle through the forms and swung the weapon around a bit. It looked like he was enjoying himself.

"Truly, this is a splendid job. How much do I owe you?"

"Nah, don't worry about that. Just help me out if those jokers ever give me trouble again."

"Very well, then. It's a promise." Neil let out a gentle laugh as he spoke. *Well, I'm sure those guys won't be stupid enough to try anything again.*

"...You guys were warned about this yesterday!" I was wrong. They were stupid enough.

The moonlight illuminated the garden outside my home, highlighting around fifty armed intruders who were now flat out on the ground. Blondie, Brown-hair, and Redhead were with them. The rest were fairly large, well-built men. Probably mercenaries or personal soldiers.

Lapis had informed me that a mob of suspicious individuals was making its way toward my home, so I had Tom pretend to be asleep at the gate. Lapis was a member of Espion after all, an elite spy that answered directly to the royal family. Her information was bang on the mark, so I was ready when the mob swarmed through and spilled into the garden under the cover of night.

They were surprised to see me waiting for them, but it didn't take them long to try to jump me at once when they realized I was all alone. At that point it was a simple matter of firing off fifty paralyzing rounds. Honestly, I was extremely disappointed. Even Lone-Horned Wolves had more impressive movements than those chumps.

"Did you just completely ignore what Neil told you?" I approached Blondie, who was practically glued to the ground. I then squatted down and smacked his shoulder with Brunhild a couple of times. He couldn't move due to the paralysis, but he was still conscious, so he'd be able to hear my words. That much was clear by the fear I could see in his eyes.

"Do you even understand your situation? You've got your weapons hanging right there on your sides. This is clearly a raid, isn't it? So what you've got here is attempted robbery, attempted assault, most likely attempted murder, right? Well, not like that matters now."

"Is everything alright now, Touya?" Yumina walked out on to the terrace, and Blondie's eyes went wide with confusion. *Heheh... I'm glad that even a moron like this guy can recognize Yumina. That's good, it'll make things go much smoother.*

"Well, do you get it now? What you've committed is high treason, an act against royalty! And because of your idiocy, your noble houses are all going to come crashing down. Beheadings for all! Good work, guys. Really. You nailed it." Blondie listened to me until he could bear no more and passed out, frothing slightly at the mouth. It was just a threat, but... I still couldn't believe he'd reacted like that.

I asked Tom to take the bicycle and forward a message to the knight order on my behalf.

"What are you going to do with them?"

"Well, nobody got hurt, so I don't think executing them is really justified... Still, this crime will definitely follow back to their families. They may even be stripped of their noble status. Regardless of what happens, these individuals will never see high status or praise again in their lives." If you asked me, they got what was coming to them, and their families would too. The fact remained that their parents knew about their misdeeds and kept protecting them regardless. Neil even tried to warn them, but they ignored him completely... They really should never have tried attacking me again. Bunch of morons.

I figured that they'd intended to strike in the night and outnumber us to gain the upper hand. Then, come morning, they'd pretend what happened was just a robbery gone wrong or something... It really irritated me to think about, actually.

They were like petulant kids who couldn't see the future consequences of their own actions. Didn't their parents ever teach them any respect? It was probably their fault for raising such trashy kids. If they'd been better parents, maybe their kids wouldn't have turned out to be such idiots.

All of the intruders were apprehended when Tom returned with a group of knights. *Good riddance,* I thought. *Hope I never see you again.*

A few days later, some of the noble houses were stripped of their lands and status. It was a direct decree from the king, apparently.

The knight order was shamed by the incident, and pledged to crack down with disciplinary measures. From that day onward, social status was irrelevant within their ranks.

"Hm… it didn't turn out 3D after all, then?" I pensively looked over the projected image. I had expected a three-dimensional image to come up, but it wasn't to be.

It was the product of a recently acquired Null spell, [**Mirage**]. To sum it up briefly, it was a spell that allowed me to conjure illusions.

I had first tested it out by making an illusory version of Kohaku, and it actually looked like the real thing from every angle I stood at. I was also able to control the movements of the image, but I couldn't physically touch it. It was just light, after all. I thought about using it to project a ghost, but that would've been way too scary. It would've been creepy if one of these peeked at you through a wall, too.

I was curious about what would happen if I enchanted my smartphone's video player with [**Mirage**], so I gave it a shot.

"Hmm… well, it's fine from the front." My phone was now magically projecting a cartoon into the air in the middle of the room. When I looked at the projection from the side, it was no good at all, though. Just a flat bit of light. It seems like enchanting my phone's video app with [**Mirage**] only served to turn it into a projector. But still, that was an impressive feat in itself.

"Hmm… so it doesn't scan the whole video and make it a 3D scene or anything… That's a shame. Guess it's just a regular old projector, then." Just as I was losing myself in thought, I heard a loud rapping on the door.

"Touya, bruv. I brought you some lun— What the bloody hell is that?!" Renne came into the room, suddenly stopping in her tracks to stare wide-eyed at the cartoon suspended in the air. Kohaku came up alongside her, and he too seemed curiously amazed. Well, I wasn't too surprised by their shock.

"Oi, oi. Bruv, what's that thing?!"

"Oh uh… It's a moving picture show. I'm projecting it into the air with magic."

"Wow…!" I could almost see the stars in Renne's eyes as she gazed at the hologram. The cartoon on show was an old foreign show about a pair of animals that chased each other around. It had little to no dialogue, so it was simple enough to just sit back and enjoy.

Renne sat down on a chair, her eyes transfixed on the cartoon. She'd already slumped down into the "I'm not moving from this position any time soon" posture. The episodes were brief, so it wasn't like I minded her taking a little break from things. I suddenly turned to find Kohaku, slack-jawed and wide-eyed, gazing over at the cartoon as well. What a silly tiger.

They seemed to be completely fine with stuff like vacuum cleaners and refrigerators showing up in the cartoon, but I guess they didn't need to know what they were to understand. The people of this world would probably just consider them to be "magical tools" or something to that effect.

Before long, just as the episode was drawing to a close, I heard another knock at the door. *I've got a bad feeling about this…*

"Heyyy sir. Have you seeeeen sweet little Renneeee around— Wow! Wooow! What is thaaat?!" Cecile opened the door and quickly came barging in. *Well, this can only end well.* Just as I'd expected, Cecile plonked herself down next to Renne and began to watch the show.

After the episode finished, it was Kohaku of all people who turned to me with a pleading expression. It was a face that said "More please." I reluctantly set the phone to automatically play new episodes when the previous finished, then went to fix up some lunch. I was fine leaving my smartphone alone, because I'd applied a **[Program]** to it that allowed me to recall it to my hand at will. It's a combined enchantment that makes use of [**Gate**] and [**Apport**]. A simple, but effective anti-theft measure.

Everyone out on the terrace had already started to eat. The lunch of the day was onion soup, club sandwiches, and a veggie salad with cheese.

I arrived at the table and prepared to eat. Sure looked tasty. First thing I grabbed was a club sandwich, which I stuffed into my cheeks, savoring the flavor. It tasted as excellent as it looked. The chicken was juicy, and the tomato was flavorful. There wasn't much more I could ask for, really.

"What are Renne and Cecile up to?" Lapis pondered the whereabouts of the two absentees as she poured juice into my glass. I didn't want her to get mad at them, so I decided I'd have her fall into the same trap that they had succumbed to.

"They're currently helping me out a bit with my magic. Actually, Lapis, since you're done here and all… you should head over to my room and see them."

"Hm…?" Lapis headed back inside with a curious look on her face. I knew that as soon as she laid eyes upon the cartoon, she'd be unable to escape its snare.

"So Touya, what're you doing today?" Elze cut in, talking to me while sipping her post-meal tea.

"Well, I'll be heading to Eashen in a bit because Yae's weapon should be done today. I'll go and speak to her parents while I'm there, as well. After that, I'll be going to see your uncle."

"Oh, you can feel free to put off going to see our family, Touya. If our aunt found out we'd be getting married to the same man as the princess of Belfast she'd have a heart attack." Elze and Linze hailed from the Refreese Imperium, a country just west of Belfast. They were raised on a farm by their aunt and uncle in the village of Saletto, in the eastern part of Refreese. As I understood it, their real parents died of illness when both of the girls were young...

"Don't be silly, I'll have to talk to them eventually. We'll take some flowers to the grave of your parents while we're there, too."

"...Th-Thank you, Touya." Linze smiled from across the table, apparently feeling both timid and happy.

"Now, shall we check up on our lovely maid trio?" After the meal, I took the others up to the bedroom. As I had expected, all three of the maids were completely engrossed in the cartoon. Kohaku was curled up in Renne's lap, purring gently as the action unfolded.

Elze and the others became glued to the screen pretty quickly too. I turned it off after the episode finished running. It *did* have to end sometime, after all.

Everyone started to complain, but I quickly diffused the growing storm by promising to put it back on after dinner that evening. That, thankfully, appeased them.

It became increasingly clear to me that the people of this world were starved for entertainment. Indeed, after one reached adulthood, it was a considerably larger amount of work, and a considerably lesser amount of play. But, in a world like this one, there were a lot of things that needed to be done in order to survive, so it might've just been that they simply didn't have time to enjoy themselves.

After that, I took Yae off with me to Eashen, and we approached the smithy that we'd visited the last time.

"Hey there, we're here to pick up a katana?"

"Oh, hey there! Yup, as promised, your order's ready and waitin'." The smith came out from the back of the store, holding a katana in one hand and a short blade in the other. They were both sheathed in beautiful crimson sheaths.

Yae accepted the weapons, then swiftly unsheathed them. It seemed like she was eager to look them over. The blade shone a brilliant silver, and I could see a finely adorned pattern dancing along it.

"It is extremely light… I suppose that is what you would expect from a mithril weapon, yes." Yae made a few standard swings with the weapon in order to get a good feel for it, and then she sheathed the blade. She suddenly crouched down, gathering her center of gravity, and drew the blade from her hip with a slash. *She's fast!*

"It flows very well. This is a wonderful blade, it is."

"Thanks a bunch." The smith smiled a bit at Yae's compliment. It seemed that he was a very talented man after all.

I cast [**Storage**] and pulled out a hunk of mithril to pay him with. I pulled out around twice the amount of mithril I had initially given him to forge the weaponry with. As I moved to hand it over to him, the smith looked at me with wide-eyed shock.

"Hey, hey… ain't this a little much?"

"Don't worry about it. I might want to use your services again in the future, so just work as hard as you did this time and we'll get along just fine."

"…Fair enough. Well, if ya really don't mind, I'll be taking it, then."

The smith let out a jovial laugh, his mithril chunk in hand. Yae and I bid him farewell, then headed off on our way.

Once we got back to the mansion, it was time for dinner. Once we wolfed down our food, it was holo-vision time. The girls all hurried me into my room, but I still had enough willpower to limit them to three hours.

I turned out all the lights so the audience could better see the projection. The show I had chosen this time was an animation, much like before, except this one was about an hour long. I chose a fantasy story rather than a modern-day drama, because it would be easier for the citizens of the other world to identify with.

Elze, Linze, Yae, Yumina, Lapis, Cecile, Renne, Cesca, Julio, Crea, and Leim were all packed into my room. My beastly trio, consisting of Sango, Kokuyou, and Kohaku, had also decided to attend the screening. I found it almost cute, like a little cinema. Sadly, Tom and Huck had to stay on guard duty, so they were unable to attend. I made a mental note to make it up to them both later.

Everyone was completely captivated by what they were watching. I had always figured that this other world had little in the way of entertainment, but I never stopped to think about it, really. They probably didn't even have team sports like soccer or baseball. They certainly didn't have anything like video games or cartoons, for sure. The knights of Belfast had their mock battles, but that was more for training purposes than entertainment.

*Come to think of it... if they don't have a large sports culture, does that mean they don't have athletic festivals or sports days, either? The kids in town race each other sometimes, so they at least know stuff like that as a concept... But I wonder if they've ever experienced a relay race, or an obstacle course, or a bread-eating contest! They could even do that game where three guys lift up another guy and try to knock down the enemy guy. Like a mock cavalry charge... Actually, the people here could probably organize a real cavalry charge. It'd be pretty nice if the townspeople could arrange something like that, getting everyone involved... We could divide the teams into red and white, too...*

Before I knew it, I was absorbed in thought, watching over the captivated audience.

"Our economy's been in a real slump lately, yeah… We've lost a lot of visitors and haven't had many guests to speak of. My dad was trying to get more business drummed up using shogi as an advertising point, but it didn't really work out." It had been a while since I last visited Reflet, so I decided to pay the Silver Moon Inn a visit. When I got there, Micah started counting her woes. I hadn't been there in a while, but I hadn't expected that they'd fall into financial hardships in such a short amount of time.

In order for an inn to profit, a guest has to stay overnight. In order for a guest to stay overnight, the town has to have some sort of attraction. I guess Reflet just… wasn't all that interesting, it didn't really have anything to make it stand out as a tourism hotspot.

*Now if this place had a hot spring, that'd be another story entirely.*

*Maybe we could dig one up…? Nah, pretty sure you need to be in a volcanic area for a hot spring to even be possible…*

"Are there no town events going on any time soon? A festival, maybe?"

"… Nope. What kind of festival do you mean?"

"Uhh, well… I can't really think up a festival on the spot like that. My home country has the Snow Festival, or Tanabata… How about something like that?"

"It doesn't really snow here… and what's a tan batter?" *Nah, this won't work either. Even if we put on a festival, it'd be a temporary solution. Sure, the place would be bustling with tourists for a while, but that would only be for one short period a year. The rest of the time the place would be a regular ghost town…*

I decided that the best thing to do to attract customers would be to give the Silver Moon something only it could have. Really, installing hot springs would be the ideal in this situation. With that in place, tourists from miles around would surely flock to the Silver Moon.

*Can I make an artificial hot spring if I boil water with magic…? Ah, wait… I'd have to boil it every day, so that wouldn't be very efficient. It wouldn't really be much of a hot spring, either… Is there anything else I can do here? Wait… I've got it!* "… A hot spring! I'll make one for you, Micah."

"Wh-What?" *Yeah, I can make one. It'll actually be pretty easy to make one! All I'd have to do is go to a natural hot spring, pull some hot water through with a* **[Gate]***, let it flow through, then drain it out with another* **[Gate]***. No big deal at all.*

"Can you really make one?"

"It should be possible, yeah. It probably won't take a lot of time, either."

"If you could make one, it'd be amazing… Uhm, what can I do to help?" Just as Micah started to fire herself up, Dolan wandered in. Dolan raised his brow in excitement upon hearing the mention of a hot spring, and quickly confirmed the story so far.

"So you're saying you can make us a hot spring by connecting a far-off one to our little Inn?!"

"Well, yeah. Probably. I can definitely give it a shot." I pulled up my smartphone and ran a search for "hot springs." There was one on the outskirts of the Melicia Mountains, in a forested area to the south. I asked Micah, just to be sure, but she said she'd never heard of a place like that. Seemed like it was a secluded one that few knew about. That was more than perfect for me.

I used [Gate] to head back to the garden, taking Cesca along with me. Together, we sailed off in the skies toward the spot on the map.

"Master… you'd really go so far as to take me into a secluded mountain hot spring, just to see me in the nude…? You know that all you have to do is give the order and I'd drop my panties like they're hot, right?"

"I don't have any intentions like that! Stop lifting that skirt!" I karate chopped the robo-brat in a vain attempt to end her sexual harassment. That girl had too many lewd scenarios in her head, it was troublesome.

Eventually the garden arrived at its destination, I disembarked. *Oho, I can smell it… This is the smell of a hot spring.*

I made my way through the bushes and found the natural spring within a forest glade. The water looked great, it didn't have any grime or impurities in it at all. I got closer and dipped my hand into the water. *Ouch, it's a little hot… but that's still better than it being lukewarm.*

I took a good look around, confirming multiple water sources for the spring. It seemed that quantity wouldn't be an issue, either.

I decided to install a pipe enchanted with [Gate] connected to another enchanted set of piping at the Silver Moon. This would allow water to flow from here to there, and back again. The Silver Moon would become the "space" between the two pipes.

I cast [Storage] and pulled out a hunk of mithril. I decided to use that rather than iron, because the mithril wouldn't rust up. Then I created a few pipes around ten centimeters in diameter, and thirty centimeters in length. Then I set to work installing the piping in various areas. I used [**Modeling**] to install the pipes, so they seamlessly fit together.

"Alright, everything seems ready." I used a [**Gate**] to return to Reflet... before promptly remembering that I'd left Cesca behind again.

Quickly, and thankfully, remembering my mistake, I stepped through another portal and came out in the garden. I reported back to Cesca on my success.

After I made it back to the Silver Moon, I walked around their backyard looking for a good spot. I dug out a water channel with magic about 30 centimeters deep. It was also about one meter long in total. I reinforced the waterway with stone to prevent the water from getting all muddy and gross.

Then, using [**Storage**] again, I pulled out some mithril and began work on the next pipe. I then crafted an ornate lion's head and fixed it over one end of the waterway, its mouth serving as the spout. I realized that if I enchanted it with [**Gate**] right away, then water would come flying out of it uncontrollably.

To counter that, I used [**Program**] to set the portal to open or close based on whether a nearby person gave the keyword "Open" or "Close." That way the flow of water could easily be controlled. I kept it closed for the time being, and lodged another mithril pipe slightly higher up on the other side of the little hole I'd made. The hot water would flow into the spring from the lower pipe, and then flow out through the higher pipe, heading through a portal back to where it came from. One would supply the water, the other would work as a drain.

"I think everything should be in order now." I spoke the keyword "Open," and hot water began to flow out of the lion's mouth. Micah and Dolan looked on with amazement. "Whoa!"

"Wow! It's really a hot water spout?!" The hot water spilled from the ornate lion's mouth, and began to fill up the little waterway. When the water level reached the hole on the other side, the depth remained level. The hot water that poured into the hole would flow back into the springs near the mountains, creating an even loop.

I kicked off my footwear and splashed my feet around in the water a bit. *Yowch, a little hot, but it actually feels pretty good.* "Whoa... that's amazing..."

"But does our property even have enough space for a big hot springs bath?" Dolan gazed over at the water with a look of sheer awe on his face, while Micah pondered a serious issue. Luckily for her, I'd already pondered that for her.

"Correct me if I'm wrong, but that plot of land with the two homes on it is vacant, right? The ones right behind your inn."

"Er, yes it is... but what does that matter?"

"I'll buy it, then."

"What?!" It was the simplest solution, after all. I went off to the estate agency to check how much the properties were going to cost. The agent told me that the homes were eight platinum coins apiece. I paid immediately.

I had sold the broken fragments that I'd taken from the Mithril Golem, and found myself with an absolute wealth of cash as a result. I didn't need to worry about finances all that much anyway, especially when it was for a good cause.

I purchased the properties, signed the contract, and made my way back to the Silver Moon.

"Didja seriously buy those places?"

"Yup. Now, want me to renovate it all in one go?" Micah was surprised, but I still had work to do. I summoned a [**Gate**] on the flat of the ground and both homes sank into it. I had just dumped the whole lot back on my floating garden. With a swoosh, two houses vanished in an instant.

"What?!" The two were stunned. Ignoring their surprise, I continued to take out the wall that was dividing the property from the Silver Moon in the same way.

I prepared the rough outline of a bathing area using Earth magic. I spread it out pretty widely. After that, I applied some of the finer touches using [**Modeling**].

"So what about a woman's bath and a men's bath? Want me to split it into two pools?"

"Hm? Ah, yes! Can you divide it?"

"No problemo!" I divided the bath right into two halves. I surrounded them both with a rock wall, a stone pavement that lead into the washroom, some tatami mats, a roof, and a set of pillars made of cypress. Then I set up a dividing wall between the two pools. I enchanted the divider with [**Paralyze**]. That was for a little divine punishment in case any peeping Toms were skulking about.

I finished off the exterior by creating two dressing rooms and erecting long curtains for the entryways as well.

Finally, I enchanted the upper area of the bath with [**Mirage**], preventing any of the hotel guests from peeking down on it. All they would see was an image of rustling treetops. The people in the baths would see tree canopies as they looked up, as well. Nobody wants to look over and see people walking about as they bathe, after all.

All-in-all, it had become a pretty nice Japanese-style bath.

I felt a sense of pride wash over me, nodding in confirmation at my own work. Then I noticed Dolan and Micah out of the corner of my eye, both were slack-jacked and staring.

"G-Goodness… you're just full of surprises, huh…"

"You built it in no time at all…" *Well, maybe I overdid it a little. I thought it'd be a really nice idea, so I just went and did it right away. I made everything right down to the bucket and stool.*

"So wait, can we even use this bath as a business? The land and stuff is yours, right?"

"I'll lend it to you for the foreseeable future. If the place profits well enough, I'll let you buy the deed from me. It'll be sixteen platinum coins, though." I held out the proof of purchase, highlighting the amount the deed was worth. Well, the title deed was for a household property, and I had gone and replaced it with an open-air bath… I didn't think too hard about it.

"Hmhm… not bad at all. Now I can make a profit from both the lodging and the bath house… I'll make good use of it, thank you." In a world where bathing was a luxury for the upper classes and the rich, the poor were lucky to scrub themselves with a wet towel every so often. I was sure that the common folk would be extremely happy to get such a nice bath on the cheap.

"The bath won't do anything for diseases, but it should treat physical ailments pretty effectively. Bad eyes, back pain, even poison if you soak in it long enough. They should all be taken care of."

"The water really does that?" The water really did that. I had used another [**Program**] to imbue the springs with [**Recovery**]. It would cause too much of a stir if people's injuries were healed right away, so I made the spell infuse with the water, gradually applying itself over time.

We decided to open up the springs for a test run. I said the "Open" keyword for both baths, and the water began to flow. As I set everything up, Micah and Dolan went to get their friends. Today's test run would be free of charge for them all, of course.

Other than Dolan and myself, the men's bath contained Barral, the owner of the Eight-Bears Weapon Shop; Simon, the pawnbroker; and Zanac of "Fashion King Zanac" fame. *The ratio of old men to young men is way off in here!* As I was soaking up the water and getting lost in thought, the men brought a table near the water's edge. Dolan and Barrel then started to play shogi on it. *Geez, they're even playing in a place like this?*

On the women's side, other than Micah, Aer and her employees from Parent were also enjoying the soak. To my surprise, Cesca decided she'd take a dip too. *Is a robo-girl like her gonna be okay in all that water? Well… I'm sure it'll be fine, that pervy doctor wouldn't make an oversight like that.*

"Master, shall I wash your back?"

"Don't say stupid stuff! Just be quiet and enjoy the bath!" I angrily yelled over the wall at Cesca. *How inappropriate does she want to be?!* "Now now, don't be so shy, master…"

"C-Cesca! What are you climbing up there for?!"

"Fhgyh?!" I heard Micah call out for that idiot, then I heard Cesca's muffled voice, shortly followed by a "splash" as something fell into the women's bath. That was interesting, so [**Paralysis**] even worked on a being like her. Then again, she did mention having biological parts.

"If you try to scale the wall for some peeping, there'll be a world of hurt in it for you. Just so we're clear." I explained the system to the men who were in the bath with me, they all nodded their heads in obedience. That said, I never expected the first offender to come from the female side…

With the pest out of the way, I was free to enjoy the relaxing hot water. *Ah… feels so good.*

"I'll be straightforward. You all like Touya, don't you?" Facing Elze, Linze, and Yae, Yumina said exactly what was on her mind. While they were examining the new home they'd received from the king of Belfast, she asked that question after having called the three to a balcony on the second floor. The girls became flustered and red to their ears.

"I-It's not like I *like* him or anything! I-I-I mean, he's so unreliable and soft-hearted! W-Well, he's kind, so it's not like he doesn't have any good points, but… No, I mean that—"

"But Elze, you often look at the clothes he bought you and always seem so happy while doing it. I even saw you hugging them tight once."

"Ugh?!" Likely never having thought that someone had seen her, Elze grew even redder.

"You too, Linze. Last day off, you were stalking him, weren't you?"

"Fhyahh?! I-I-I-I was just, umm… I wanted to know where he was going! When I thought that it might've been a brothel, I just couldn't help it…!" Flustered more than ever, Linze shook her hands as she explained.

"And that got you following him for a whole day, hm?"

"Uohh…" Linze bashfully hung her head.

Her elder twin sister was unaware of this, so she looked at Linze with eyes full of shock. Unable to bear it, she crouched down and put her hands over her reddened face.

"And you, Yae…"

"N-No, I do not think anything of him, I do not…"

"Really? What about the times when you get hurt in battle? You always ask for Touya to heal you, right? Linze can do it too, you know?"

"Th-That is just…" Linze looked at Yae, who shifted her gaze away and made it all too obvious. In response, Yumina smiled.

"I don't find that unpleasant in the least. In fact, it makes me happy. After all, it means that, other than me, there are three people who believe in and support Touya with all they are."

"…That's just weird. Most people wouldn't like it, right?"

"Really? Let me make it clear. Touya is a person who's going to do great things soon. Keeping such a man all to myself would be far stranger. There are things I can't support him with on my own, after all. Reasons like 'I want him to be mine alone' are far too insignificant to let myself bind a person like him to me." Yumina replied to Elze's words as if it wasn't a big deal. It wasn't like she didn't want to have him all to herself, but Yumina was more afraid of narrowing his possibilities.

Also, the three girls before her were deserving of her trust. They loved the same man as her, and would support him with all they had. With that in mind, she suggested something.

"So, how about we all become his wives?"

"Wh-What?!" All the girls looked up in wide-eyed shock.

I'd always had an inferiority complex about my little sister. Ever since I was small, I'd been called 'thuggish' and 'unladylike' when compared to her.

It was true that my little sister was cute. Considering I was her twin, that might have sounded like I was merely praising myself, but she was 'a girl' in every sense of the word.

There was no denying that she was a bit introverted and afraid of strangers, but that could actually work in her favor by triggering a man's desire to protect her.

She could also cook and was gifted with magic talents. Also, her b-breasts were far bigger than mine… Since she and I were twins, I always felt that God was a bit unfair to me in that regard.

I grew out my hair as an attempt to be more feminine, but that didn't affect who I was on the inside. Everyone still always called me 'mannish' or 'violent.'

In fact, when we lived in the countryside, I was the strongest person out of everyone my age. I used to knock out anyone who made my little sister cry, so it was only obvious that they wouldn't see me as a 'girl.'

However, Touya was different. He saw me as a girl the very moment we met. And, unlike the boys in the countryside, he was very kind. Not to mention that he'd been considerate about the smallest things and shown concern whenever he had to.

Touya made me very happy when he bought me some cute clothes. I never thought that I'd have a boy tell me that clothes like that looked good on me. For one reason or another, simply remembering it made me smile, which perplexed me to no end. Though it was a mysterious feeling, I didn't dislike it at all.

Little by little, I became more and more interested in him. And before I knew it, I began looking at him wherever he went. Clearly, it was too late at that point.

*I probably love him.* I used 'probably' because I'd never felt that way before.

The boys that surrounded me were either little brother figures or the enemies bullying my little sister. However, by the time I grew aware of my feelings, Yumina was already with us. She was smart, proactive, had a talent for magic, and was even a princess — a 'girl' to the point it was unfair. I simply had no chance against her. With that excuse as a weight, I bound my feelings and hid them deep within my heart.

That was why I panicked when Yumina saw right through me. I didn't really care about being his lover — I could be at his side by being a friend and an ally in battle. I was even about to make peace with that idea.

Being her twin, I had a hunch that Linze also had similar feelings for him. Though, I was a bit surprised to know that Yae felt that way, too.

Yumina's suggestion took me straight from being surprised to making my mind go blank.

*I mean... a wife? Me? T-Touya's wife?* Did that mean that I'd have to marry him?! That was a necessary part of it, right?! I loved Touya, yes, but wasn't that a bit too sudden?! I didn't know if I was even mentally prepared for that! And even if I was okay with it, I didn't know if Touya would be! *Wh-What should I do...?!*

I'd always been a timid person. Constantly hiding behind my big sister, I never said anything I wanted to. When faced with people I didn't know, I grew tense to the point of making my words awkward and rendering me unable to have a proper exchange.

Unlike me, my big sister never got scared. She was always frank, and quickly became friends with anyone. I'd always been envious of that side of her.

Ever since I was young, I was troubled by this and wondered why we were so different despite being twins. If my sister was the sun, I was the moon. The moon couldn't even shine without the sun's light. Without her, I couldn't do anything. And I hated myself for it.

That was probably the reason why, when I was a child, the boys around me would get angry and bully me. Though, most of the ones who did that would end up getting punched by Elze.

Because of that, I was never comfortable around boys. That went double for boys my age. I never knew what to say when I was with them, causing me to always turn silent.

My first impression of Touya was that he 'seemed like a kind person.' Despite that, I wasn't able to have a proper conversation with him.

Even when he asked me to teach him about magic, I was worried if I could actually do it properly and got all tense, making my explanation sound awkward. However, rather than getting angry at me, Touya listened and was really impressed by what I told him. Before I knew it, I was at ease.

Since then, Touya couldn't stop surprising me. He had an affinity for all types of magic, taught us about ice cream, and had a… smartfoan. Plus, just recently, he even saved the king's life.

As I spent more time with him, I eventually became able to interact with him like I would interact with a normal friend.

However, soon after that, it became hard again.

When talking to him or whenever he would praise me, my heart would begin to race and cause me to stutter. I didn't know why that was happening, but when he came back with Yumina at his side, I felt a pain in my chest. That was how I became aware of my feelings.

However, I couldn't do anything about them. Despite being younger than me, Yumina was proactive and decisive, making her a good match for Touya. It made me sad when I had to think that I'd have to watch over them while hiding my true feelings.

But Yumina herself, seemingly thinking of Touya more than anyone else, told me to join her in being Touya's wife. Not only that, but Sis and Yae would be with us, too. I couldn't wrap my head around it…

But if that happened… I'd have been happy beyond words. After all, I would be able to be at Touya's side, too.

*B-But that means that we'll have to get married, right? M-Marriage?!* That word alone was enough to make me turn beet red.

*Hawah, hawawah… Me and Touya? Together?! I'm happy! Very happy, but…!* But I still didn't know if Touya would accept me. In fact, I didn't even know how to control my feelings on the matter.

Was it really okay for this to happen…? For Touya and me to get married…? *Hawah… Awawawah…*

I had held the blade for as long as I could remember, I had. Since I was young, I would spend each and every day training with my father and brother.

Training and sword-fighting was always a fun thing to do, it was. Swinging swords always set my mind at ease, after all. There was nothing more pleasant than the moment when I became one with the well-honed sword in my hands and entered a trance-like state. The only ones who could relate to that were my father and brother. My mother and our house servant, Ayane, would always tell me to be more reserved and feminine.

After I left Eashen and began training in other countries, I eventually reached the Kingdom of Belfast. This was the land where I met Touya-dono and the others.

It all began when he helped me deal with some outlaws. At first, I thought that he was from Eashen, just like myself, but that turned out to not be the case. It immediately made him a mysterious person to me, it did.

Touya-dono's swordplay was quite strange. Well, he was peculiar in many other aspects, but what mystified me the most was that, despite having the posture and swing of a beginner, he was curiously strong. He was likely blessed with an exceptionally good basic movement ability and kinetic vision that allowed him to better perceive the things around him.

As proof of that, he was able to copy my swinging and movements after only a short spar against me. A beginner's technique mixed with formidable natural talent. As a swordsman, Touya-dono was truly strange.

I found that unbalanced technique of his to be quite interesting and even somewhat amusing, but eventually, I grew to become more excited about talking to him than I was about sparring with him. Back then, I tried to convince myself that I simply felt an affinity to him due his mentality and many of his likes being similar to that of an Eashen man.

At first glance, Touya-dono did not seem strong in the least, he did not. However, he had the strength to face anything as long as it was for the sake of what he wished to protect... Just like my brother.

He could struggle for the sake of someone other than himself. As if it was obvious, he extended his hand to anyone who needed help. Once I realized that was simply part of his nature, it was far too late. To my own shock, I began following him with my gaze and was unable to compose myself whenever we were sparring or simply talking.

However, Touya-dono already had a fiancee — Yumina-dono. Thus, I began to believe that my feelings would never reach him.

I never would have thought that I, alongside Elze-dono and Linze-dono, would be offered the position of Touya-dono's brides.

*How am I to respond to this...?* The pure happiness I felt was mixed with bewilderment and making my head spin.

*To become his bride obviously means that I would be his w-w-wife...! And Touya-dono would be my husband... A husband! I-Is that not a bit too sudden, is it not?! H-Hmm...*

"H-How am I supposed to react to that...?"

"Umm, I... Ohh..."

"Hmmm..." The three became beet red and let their gazes wander. It was easy to tell that they weren't averse to the idea, at least. Yumina was pleased with the reaction and smiled broadly.

"I guess this *is* a bit sudden. Well then, let's put this subject aside until you three are sure about how you feel." She put her hands together and gave that suggestion. After all, forcing them into it might've made them get stubborn in some strange way.

"That aside, you're all planning on living here, right?"

"W-Well… if Touya is alright with it…"

"No need to worry about that. Touya said it himself, didn't he? 'I like you all as much as the other. You're like family to me.' Though, it's a bit sad that he called us 'family' rather than treating us like proper women." Yumina's words made Linze think. If they were to get married and become husband and wife, wouldn't they have been family, anyway?

And so, the four girls formed a secret agreement.

And, a few months later…

"Well, now that things are made clear and we all became Touya's fiancees…" The night Touya accepted their feelings, the girls all gathered in Yumina's room and began a meeting. Eventually, such events would come to be called 'Wife Meetings,' but that didn't matter right now.

By the way, their beloved was out cold due to Elze's punch and was now lying on his bed.

"As you are all aware, Touya's powers are far beyond the norm. As he has done until now, he will continue using them to save many people. However, there could be some who would try to use his powers for their own gain." In response to Yumina's words Yae folded her arms and nodded.

"That is true. Touya-dono seems to be dense when it comes to his own worth."

"He is soft-hearted, after all. People like him are easy to fool."

"I can easily see through such sorts with my Mystic Eye, so there's no need to worry about them. The problem is with harmful results of goodwill." Elze's words made Yumina turn slightly sad. In response, Linze asked for an elaboration.

"…Wh-What do you mean?"

"Let's say there's a woman that loves Touya. What if the people surrounding her — such as her parents, siblings, other relatives, or simply friends — wanted to use Touya and demanded that she did something unreasonable? What if she went and begged Touya to help her with it? Now, do you think he'd be able to refuse, even if he knew that he could get hurt in the process?" Yumina's Mystic Eyes of Intuition could see the true nature of people. But even if their true nature was good, there was no guarantee that their actions would be. Acts born out of good intentions could always result in something terrible.

"The scariest scenario would be one where the person is in the same position as us."

"A fiancee, you mean?"

"Yes. I believe that there will be more people who will fall in love with Touya. With that, there might… No, there *will* be more fiancees. When that happens, I don't want them to be people who would pick their family's interests and advantages over what's best for Touya." Marriage between nobles was simply the joining of the families. Such politicized marriage wasn't uncommon in the least, and brides who married only for their own family, rather than the groom's, were many.

Yumina had absolutely no intention of accepting someone like that. Even if the girl liked Touya, she had to put him above all else. Otherwise, she'd soon be nothing but a burden. Yumina didn't think for a second that she could get along with such women.

Though she was the princess of Belfast, if her father ever told her to have Touya do something dangerous for the sake of the kingdom, she would never comply.

"Women who'd prioritize their own family over Touya, huh…? I imagine there's tons of noble ladies like that…" Elze muttered.

"I have no confidence that I would be able to get along with such people… Though, would there really be more fiancees, would there…?"

"I believe so. Sue is a strong candidate and might join us in two or so years. Not that there would be many problems with her."

"Oh, that's true. She's really fond of him. Though, it's more like a sibling relationship at this point." Yumina wasn't averse to the idea of Sue wanting to get married to Touya. And the girl's father, Duke Ortlinde, wasn't the type to use Touya to further his family.

However, there was no guarantee that there wouldn't be any nobles who would marry off their daughters to Touya just for personal gain. That wasn't limited to Belfast, either. There could be marriage proposals coming from other countries, such as Mismede and Refreese.

Yumina believed that she and the other girls could prevent such things from happening. For a while, they could reject such proposals by simply saying that there were already four of them. However, as Touya's fame would increase, so would the possibility of there being more fiancees. Of course, if the new girls thought of Touya above all else, they wouldn't mind them joining even if they were nobles or princesses from other countries.

"For now, however, Touya will have to be supported by just the four of us. To do that, we have to become powerful, as well. Powerful enough to walk this life at his side, that is."

"True. He can be really unreliable at times."

"I-I-I'll do my best!"

"But what is it we can do at this point in time?" Yae slightly tilted her head. She didn't know what she could do for his sake. A girl like her, who spent her entire life following the path of the sword, simply didn't have anything in mind.

"There's no need to overthink it. You only need to try to become someone dear to him. Since we're all fiancees now, perhaps we should try getting closer to him."

"C-C-Closer, as in…?"

"Holding his hand, linking your arms with his, hugging him. Start with a little physical intimacy, basically." Yumina's words made the other girls turn beet red. The purity on display in that reaction made the princess smile. However, at that point, she herself wasn't able to be that clingy and kept her physical limits with Touya at about the same as Sue's.

Though there were many difficulties ahead of them, Yumina was confident that she and the other girls would do just fine. After all… you couldn't hurry love, no, you just had to wait.

Interlude II:
**The Cursed Sea**

"This thing can go pretty fast."

"Well, that's because the garden doesn't have any unnecessary facilities, unlike the other Babylons." The floating garden silently streamed above the clouds like a boat. Thanks to the surrounding magical barrier, in spite of the garden moving at an impressive speed, we only felt a slight breeze on board.

Another curiosity of the barrier was that if, say, a bird were to collide with the garden, the bird would instead be teleported behind it. The lack of exploding birds was indeed a welcome feature.

Cesca, the manager of the garden, operated it using a black monolithic device installed in the center of the vessel. As Cesca touched different places on the touch panel-like device, glowing red letters would appear and disappear.

Linze and Yumina watched in awe from either side. Similarly, the floating Sango and Kokuyou gazed at the monolith as well.

"Are you the only one who can operate this thing, Cesca?"

"The only other one who's allowed is Master. Though that's more who may operate it, rather than who can, I suppose." Cesca answered Linze's question without moving her hands away from the monolith.

"Is this vessel for recreation? Since it's called the garden and all." In response to my question, Cesca wagged her finger at me with a tut-tut. *What's her problem? That's really irritating.*

"Just take a look at that flower by master's feet."

"Hmm? These?" I looked down at my feet as told, and sure enough, there was a small, yellow, bell-shaped flower blooming.

It kinda looked like a sandersonia. Except there was only one of them.

"That's called moonbeam grass, an ingredient in potions for treating mana starvation. And that flower over there is called sunbeam grass. It's an ingredient in potions for recovering stamina. All the flowers in the garden are medicinal plants with their own characteristics."

*That's amazing. Guess it really isn't an ordinary garden. It's kind of odd how quickly just hearing that explanation turned my impression around. So a lot of different drugs can be made here, huh?*

"Well, I've got no idea how you formulate any of those drugs, though."

"Huh?! You can't make them?!"

"That'd fall under the alchemy department's jurisdiction. Or maybe you could look it up in the library. Each Babylon's been specialized to the point where a single one by itself isn't all that useful." *Seriously?* That didn't sound very convenient.

As I thought that information over, a map and some text appeared on the monolith that seemed to catch Cesca's attention.

"What's wrong?"

"I'm getting an unusual magical reading. It's down below. Maybe a special kind of magical beast?"

"Down below? Where, exactly?"

"A sea to the west of the Kingdom of Belfast. Let's go take a look." And with that said, the garden silently began to dive into the sea of clouds, rapidly descending to the sea below.

The weather below the clouds was gloomy, the air saturated with a dim mist. Though none of it entered the garden thanks to the magic barrier.

"Hey, did something happen?"

"The clouds are quite thick, they are." Elze, Yae, and Kohaku noticed the Babylon's sudden rapid descent and paused their training to come this way.

"There was some sort of weird magical reading, apparently."

"Magical reading? Could it possibly be another Babylon, could it?"

"Nope. A Babylon's barrier should completely isolate its mana signature from the outside world. It's most likely either a magical beast or artifact."

*So a magical beast of the sea, maybe?* If it lived in the sea, it'd probably be something huge. Like a kraken or a killer whale, maybe. *Oh, if it's a sea-dweller...*

"Sango, Kokuyou. Anything you guys can figure out?"

"No, I do sense sseveral readings, but no ssstrange magical beastss in particular."

"No, my lord. There don't seem to be any particularly strange ones in the sea. Maybe there's one in the air?" I thought Sango and Kokuyou would've known if it were an aquatic magical beast. So maybe it was something else? Like some sort of artifact swept out to sea.

"T-Touya, look at that!" Yumina shouted as she looked down at the sea from the garden's edge. Incidentally, she wasn't in any danger since the magical shield would've prevented her from accidentally falling off the Babylon.

I followed her pointing finger to find a single boat floating through the mist. It was rusted here and there, and barnacles crusted its hull. Tattered sails hung off its three masts. And lining its deck were rusted cannons.

Ominous light emanated from the tattered ship as it silently drifted in the sea.

It was obviously in pretty bad condition. The fact that it was still even floating was nothing less than a miracle, actually.

"A ghost ship...?" I questioned.

"G-Ghost ship?!" Elze loudly echoed my whisper. Yae, who was standing next to her, turned pale as she cast her gaze to the sea.

Conversely, Linze remained calm. She had a pensive hand placed upon her chin.

"Is it really a ghost ship, though? Maybe it's just been abandoned recently?"

"Well, if you think about it rationally, I guess that'd make a lot more sense..." I may have been in another world, a fantasy world at that, but a ghost ship...? Really...? Then again, ghosts and wraiths and other spiritual monsters were commonplace. I'd fought the undead a few times, too.

"The magical reading's coming from over there, huh? There might be a special artifact on board that ship. Normal artifacts don't give that sort of reading, after all." That made sense, I figured. I was surprised that Cesca could tell so easily. It'd be nice to collect another artifact, but I just couldn't shake the eerie feeling that ship was giving off...

"Let's go check it out."

"Whaaat?!" Even before I could react to Linze's suggestion, Elze and Yae shouted first. Relics of the old world may have been involved, but that girl was oddly brave when it came to certain things.

"That boat may be carrying an important artifact from another country. I think it'd be best to at least check it out."

"True. We should retrieve it, and if it's dangerous, destroy it. Plus, this very well might be… Cesca, please show me the map."

"Knock yourself out." After seconding Linze's suggestion, Yumina checked the map displayed on the monolith.

"I knew it… This is the Sea of Blasphemy."

"The… Sea of Blasphemy?"

"It's a magic sea where all boats, without exception, are said to sink before they can pass through. For that reason, merchant ships and the like take long detours to avoid this area. That could explain what happened to that ship." *All boats sink there? So it's like the Bermuda Triangle in the Sargasso Sea, huh. Things like the Bermuda Triangle are a myth, but also entirely plausible in another world like this, so it's kind of scary.*

If that really was the cause of that ship's demise, then if we left it alone, it could cause another ship to sink.

"I guess we'll go check it out."

"Whaaat?!" Elze and Yae shrieked again. If we used a [Gate], we could board that ship, and with Sango and Kokuyou, we'd probably be able to manage with the sea somehow.

"A-Are we really going?"

"We can't just ignore it, can we? It could cause another ship to sink, after all."

"Th-That may be true, but…" I ignored those two and opened up a [Gate]. It was easy to teleport to somewhere I could see.

"Kohaku, you stay here. Cesca, contact us through Kohaku if anything goes wrong."

"As you wish."

"Roger that, Master." I passed through the [Gate] onto the deck of the ship.

The hull's floorboards creaked ominously underfoot. The sea was gentle, but the mist only added to the eerie atmosphere of the situation.

Linze and Yumina followed me through the [**Gate**] and boarded the ship. Sango, Kokuyou, and finally Elze and Yae appeared behind me... *Why are you guys holding hands?* On the deck were cannons jutting out the side of the ship as well as small boards. The cannons were obviously rusted, and the boards were rotten and clearly useless.

The floorboards creaked with every step. *Hopefully they don't cave in due to decay...*

"Doesn't look like anyone's on deck." Linze was right. Just one cursory glance revealed that not a soul was on deck.

It was like that one ship, the San Juan Bautista. The first Japanese-built Western-style sailing ship built by Date Masamune, the first daimyo of Sendai. Hasekura Tsunenaga sailed it to Spain as a diplomat. It had been restored and should still have been on display in Ishinomaki. My grandpa took me there to see it once.

According to a little smartphone research, this type of ship was called a galleon. If this ship had a similar layout to what I found, then the captain's cabin should've been in back. But this ship was the product of another world, so it was unlikely that every detail would be the same.

"...Now that's strange. The magical reading feels weak. It felt stronger when we were up in the air." Yumina's words made me turn still and sharpen my senses. *She's right. The magic seems to be weaker than before. Or rather, it feels like the source of the magic isn't here...*

"For now, let's just go inside. We might learn something."

"W-We're going inside?"

"W-We will stay and keep a lookout, we will. So please, go on ahead."

"...Well, that's fine by me." As Elze and Yae both put up awkward smiles, the rest of us opened the door on the rear deck.

There was a dimly-lit passage beyond it, both sides of which were lined with cannons that faced outward. I had heard that this world had cannons, but had never actually seen one. My first impression was that they seemed pretty large.

Though, I'd also heard that having a few fire wizards on board was far more efficient than using cannons. *Now that I think about it, these cannons mean that this could be an army ship. It's a bit late, but whatever.*

We passed through the rows of cannons and came across a long, thick rod protruding out of the floor.

"What's this?"

"It's the helm. It's used to make the ship turn to the sides." *So this is what a helm looks like. I always thought it would be similar to the wheel-like thing you'd see on TV...*

Anyway, since the helm was so derelict, I couldn't help but worry that pushing it a bit too hard would break it. Not that I had any intention to do that, of course. Beyond the helm, there was a door that really stood out. A lot of its decor, which likely used to be beautiful, had fallen off, and the old metallic fixings were covered in rust, but it was easy to tell that it was the door to the captain's quarters.

It was probably bent out of place, since we couldn't open it without using a bit more force. A few creaks later, we were able to get inside.

Though it was dark, I could somewhat make out the shapes of an old lantern hanging from the ceiling, a plain chair and table, and some curved blades and axes hanging on the walls.

**"Come forth, Light! Tiny Illumination: [Light Sphere]!"** Linze cast a spell that lit up the room.

On the table, I could see a sea chart, a compass, and the ship's log. And, of course, the papers had deteriorated so much that it felt like they'd crumble with just a stronger touch.

*It doesn't seem like there's anything unusual here...*

"I know it's weird saying this at this point, but this ship is pretty strange, isn't it?"

"That sure came out of left field, but why do you think that?"

"If this ship began drifting around because of some incident, you'd expect to see the crew's corpses, wouldn't you? Should we assume that they all jumped into the sea?" Yumina had a point. If it was really drifting about long enough for it to deteriorate so much, then there shouldn't have been any survivors. With that in mind, you'd expect to find a corpse or two.

*Maybe they're all piled up in a single room we didn't check yet...? That's not really something I'd like to discover, though.*

Making sure not to ruin it, I opened the old ship's log and found out that the ship belonged to pirates who pillaged Belfast's waters. My assumption that it was an army ship wasn't completely off the mark, though, since that was exactly what it was before the pirates stole it and began using it for their own dastardly deeds.

However, the dates on the log were throwing me off. *Why is the most recent entry more than a whole century old? Has this ship really been drifting about for that long...?*

"...Masster, don't you hear some sstrange ssound?"

"Huh?" Floating in the air and wrapped around Sango, as usual, Kokuyou began talking to me.

"Though, it's less of just a sound... and more of a... song?"

"A song?" Sango seemed to agree to Kokuyou's words.

I strained my ears, turned alert, and began looking around. Still, I could only hear the waves, the creaks of the boat's hull, and the fluttering of the derelict sails.

Right as I was about to say that I couldn't hear anything, the sound entered my ears.

"...re...s, we'r... pir... ...ow...of...nd ...on...f brine ...boo... we... ho..." Though I could only hear pieces of it, there was no doubt that it was what Kokuyou called it — a song.

*Wait, does that mean that this ship that's been adrift for more than a century actually has survivors on it?! There's no way!*

"Kyaaaaaahhhhhhh!" A moment later, a feminine scream reached the captain's quarters and cut my thoughts short.

"I-It's my sister and Yae!"

"Did something happen on the deck?!" We hastily ran out of the room and through the gun deck. When we got closer to the upper deck, we could hear the song clearly.

"We're pirates, we're pirates! We know naught of solid land...! Unmatched upon these waves of brine! For there's booty we must find, yo ho, hoo!" When I kicked the door open, I was greeted by a deck full of skeletons wearing pirate-like clothing and wielding cutlasses.

"This is...!" I was utterly stunned.

"Yo ho! We've got some more guests, ye bilge rats! Give 'em all a piratey welcome!"

"Aye aye, sir!" On the bow of the ship, wearing a pirate hat and an overcoat, there was a captain-like skeleton. He was accompanied by another one who also wore clothes different from the rest of the underlings — likely the first mate.

Once the skeletal captain raised his sword to the sky, the boney underlings charged at us with their own cutlasses.

"Blade mode!" I pulled out my Brunhild, turned it into a longsword, and cut down the skeletal pirates closing in on us.

Though they broke as easily as porcelain, their bones quickly began regenerating and came back together in but a moment. *Should've known that normal attacks wouldn't work on the undead.*

**"Come forth, O Light! Shining Duet: [Light Arrow]!"** I fired off three [Light Arrows] in a row, and all of them broke through a different bone pirate's head.

The undead were weak to Light magic. The three unfortunate skeletons I hit couldn't regenerate and quickly became dust.

"Look at that! A Light magic user! Been a while since someone surprised Captain Trepang like this!"

"...Trepang?"

"Aye! The ruthless devil of the seas! The one and only Captain Trepang! Yo hoo!" *A devil...? I'm pretty sure that 'trepang' is a word for 'sea cucumber,' though...*

Captain Cucumber laughed as his bones rattled. As I was wondering how to react, Yumina suddenly called out to me.

"Touya, look there!" She was pointing at the crow's nest on top of the mast, where I saw Elze and Yae, tied up and hanging on a rope.

"Sorry, they got us!"

"How careless of me..." *Oh man... Well, they couldn't use Light magic and didn't have anything that was enchanted with it, so I guess this result is only obvious.*

"Hyahahah! Don't worry, lad. After all, yer joining them soon! Except yer rope'll be goin' around yer neck and— Gah!"

"Not happening." As he rattled out some more laughs, I fired at Captain Trepang. Though I was aiming at his head, it went a bit lower and shattered his neck bone, making his skull fall to the deck.

Since the deck was tilting back and forth as the ship was being rocked by the waves, his skull began to roll around.

"Arrghhh! Me eyes be spinning! Stop me head, ye worthless bilge rats! Don't let the brine take me!" The captain's — his skull's, anyway — order made the crew hastily follow after the head.

I used that opening to cast [**Accel**], instantly went up the mast, and cut the rope holding them up.

Once they landed on the deck, Linze ran over and cut the ropes that bound them. *Okay, now there's no reason to hold back.*

"Heh, you've got stones, laddie. It takes big ones to go against me — Captain Trepang! But the price ye pay for that is heavy, indeed! Grit yer teeth, for I'm about to fillet ye like a crab!" Captain Cucumber roared that out as the first mate helped him reattach his head. ...*Fillet?*

"...Uh, vice cap'n, sir. Can you even fillet a crab...?"

"Shh! Shut up!" After a random crew member and the first mate had that exchange, Captain Cucumber shot them a glare. The two looked away from him in a highly forced manner.

"Who cares 'bout the details?! Just attack them, ya salty sea dogs!"

"Aye aye, sir!" In response to the skeletal captain's order, the bone pirates began closing in on us. It was quite a discomforting sight.

"**[Enchant]: [Cure Heal]!**" I imbued my weapon, Elze's gauntlets, and Yae's katana with Light magic. With that, their weapons should've been able to purify the undead.

"Hhaah!" Elze launched a straight punch from her right arm, blowing away the skeleton before her. Said skeleton became dust and disappeared from the ship.

Yae, too, was using her Light-imbued katana to sweep through the bones coming close to her.

Keeping up with them, I was firing Light-imbued bullets at the skeletons, destroying them one after the other. Linze was casting lances of light, while Yumina was keeping the bone pirates at bay with her wind magic. Kokuyou and Sango were firing some water projectiles as cover.

One by one, the pirates became dust, mixed with the wind, and simply disappeared.

"Oohhhhh?! Y-Yer pretty good at this!"

"I have a question. Are you the ones sinking all the ships that get close to this area?"

"Huhh? We never sunk any ships. Not a single one. Here, let me show ya." After saying that, Captain Trepang created a pale-blue, soul-like flame in his hand. It was about the size of a basketball.

As if it was some sort of call, similar flames began appearing all over the thick fog around us.

Once the fog, littered with countless such flames, began to clear, I could see more ghost ships. They rode the waves around us and were as numerous as the lights. *What the hell is this…?*

"Wait, are these all…?!" Straining my eyes, I saw that there were both war and merchant ships among them. They were all crowded with similar skeletons to the ones here, and I could see them raising their swords and the like.

*He changed all the ships that came here into ghost ships!*

"Hyahahah! I'll make yer death swift and painless! Ah, today's rum will be a blessing on these organs of mine!"

"…Vice cap'n, sir. We don't have any organs, do we?"

"Shh! I told you to shut up!" I could hear the first mate and the underling whisper to each other again. *Man, having a sea cucumber like this for a captain sounds like a pain.*

"Kheheheh! With there being so many of us… What the bilge are ya doing?" I ignored captain sea cucumber as he turned, or at least seemed to turn, looking confused, then took out my smartphone and ran a search. Obviously, it was for 'undead.' I should've done that from the start.

The map that extended as far as my sight quickly became covered in pins that marked my targets. At the same time, the sky above the undead became covered in small magic circles from the [**Multiple**] spell.

*Target locked.*

**"Strike true, Light! Sparkling Holy Lance: [Shining Javelin]!"** I cast the spell through the smartphone, making the magic circles above the undead create a rain of holy light lances.

"Gnyaaaaahhhh!"

"Ghyaaaaahhhh!"

"Goaaaaaahhhh!" Countless pirates released their final screams. After getting hit by the spears of light, one after the other, the undead became dust and disappeared from this world.

Of course, the pirates before us were no exception. I looked and saw Captain Trepang getting reduced to ash.

"Ooaghhhh?! This can't beee! What the bilge is thiiss?!" As he expressed his shock, Captain Trepang joined the rest of his crew. *Good bye, Cap'n Cucumber…*

Once the undead had all become dust, all that was left were the ships and the waves that gently caressed them.

"Well then, we're done here." As if timed for when I took a sigh of relief, an unpleasant voice rang out around us.

"Heheheh… I wouldn't be so sure about that…"

"What?!" Like a will-o'-the-wisp, a new flame appeared in the fog and came out of it with another ghost ship.

Standing on it and folding his arms was a skeletal captain wearing a differently-colored coat than Captain Trepang. In all honesty, since they were both just bones, that was the only difference I noticed. I could see more boney pirates behind him. They, too, were all holding cutlasses.

"I suggest against getting uppity just because you defeated Captain Trepang. He was the weakest captain of the 'Pirate Elite Four.' Your next opponent is me: Captain Turbanshell!"

*Turbanshell…? As in, 'turban shell'? The sea snail?! Does every pirate in these waters have a terrible naming sense?! And what the hell's the 'Pirate Elite Four' supposed to be?!*

"…What now, Touya?"

**"…Strike true, Light! Sparkling Holy Lance: [Shining Javelin]!"**

"Ughyaaaahhhhhh?!" *Goodbye, Captain Snail.*

I paid my respects to the ghost ship, which was now cleansed by Light magic. A moment later, I saw yet another pale-white flame appear, which was followed by yet another ghost ship. *Seriously? Again?!*

"Heheheh. You are now faced with another of the 'Pirate Elite Four,' Captain Seahorse! Your lives are forf—"

**"Strike true, Light! Sparkling Holy Lance: [Shining Javelin]!"**

"Fghaaaaahhhh!" *Fare thee well, Captain Seahorse.* Suddenly, another ghost ship came out of the fog and… "Heheheh… I be the—"

"Just stop already!"

"Gyoeeaahhhh!" Without even letting him name himself, I made what was probably the fourth and final captain return to dust. I didn't care what they were called. To me, they were nothing but troublesome piles of bone.

"Is that all of them?"

"Who knows? The fact that I can still feel some magic around here is pretty damn..."

"T-Touya-dono! Look there!" Yae noticed something and pointed at the fog-shrouded sea.

*Can you just stop it already...? This is getting really annoying. The same joke can only be funny three times, at most, is what I... think...*

Sure enough, the thing that appeared from the fog was a ghost ship. However, its size was different. This one was significantly larger.

In fact, it was at least four times bigger than the ship we were on. Not only that, but this one seemed to be somehow different from the others.

Standing on the bow of the ship, there was a new skeletal captain. He was clad in a crimson mantle and arrogantly spread his arms outward.

"Been a while since such good prey came along! Very well! I, the King of Pirates — Captain Wharfroach — will bring forth a bloodbath!"

*...Wharfroach? Of all things, a wharf roach? Captain wharf roach? Seriously?*

As I grew increasingly pissed with the pirates' absurd naming scheme, Captain Roach raised his black cutlass and shouted an order.

"Fire, you bilge rats!" The giant ghost ship's side, which was directed straight at us, suddenly started barraging us with cannon shots.

Cannons were basically a weapon that did nothing but fire cannonballs. Though a hit would break the ship, it would never result in an explosion.

I also heard that cannonballs fired from ships had a low accuracy and rarely landed where intended. That was why the sides of ships would be lined with many cannons and used in unison to increase the chances of landing hits.

We happened to be aboard a ghost ship, which basically put us in the palm of their hands. In fact, the ghost ship we were on was actually heading straight toward the rain of cannonballs they'd fired.

Exposed to the shots, the ship's mast broke as many holes opened up on the deck. It was already a wonder why the ship was still afloat. It had basically no endurance to speak of.

"Touya, at this rate, the ship's going to sink!"

"Khh, [Gate]!" Since Sango and Kokuyou were with us, there was no chance of us drowning, but staying on the ship was dangerous nonetheless. I opened a [Gate] on the deck and went through it to end up on Captain Roach's ship.

"Wha—?!" I materialized on the stern of the ship, behind the enemy, and used my smartphone to lock onto the undead. Spears of light rained down upon them like lightning.

"Gwaaaaaaaaarrgh!" With a final agonized scream, the skeleton pirates turned to dust. Thinking that had to be the last of them, I let my guard down. Then suddenly, there was a blade swinging down at me from behind the curtain of ashes.

"What?!" Instinctively, I flung myself down on the deck, avoiding the blade by hair's breadth. The owner of the ominous black cutlass that had nearly taken my life was none other than Captain Roach.

"Tch, almost had you there, laddie. Anyone who dies by this cutlass becomes my eternal servant."

"What'd you just say? That cutlass... Don't tell me that's the cursed Artifact?!"

"Aye. This here be the Soul Reaper, a cursed Artifact that lets me turn anyone I kill into my undead slave. But it turns its wielder into an undead too. Guess that's where the 'cursed' part comes from!" Captain Roach's jaws clacked together as he laughed heartily.

*I see now, he turned all the other captains I fought into the undead with that cutlass.* In other words, they too were victims. Brandishing his cursed blade, Captain Roach charged at me again.

**"Come forth, O Light! Shining Duet: [Light Arrow]!"**

"That ain't gonna work, lassie!" Linze fired a barrage of Light arrows at Captain Roach. But with a single wave of his red cape, the arrows all vanished before they could strike him.

*What the hell was that?! Is that what he stopped my* **[Shining Javelin]** *with earlier?!*

"Hehehe, this is a very special cape. You see, it can nullify all Light magic, which means you have no way of defeating me! Shame, ain't it, laddie?" *How kind of Captain Roach to reveal his secret to me. This guy's a moron too.*

**"Come forth, Fire! Whirling Spiral: [Fire Storm]!"**

"Kakaka, you fool! Fire magic can't hurt the undead! Even if you do scorch these old bones, they'll just regenerate!"

Captain Roach was enveloped in a whirling torrent of flames. But they burnt out quickly, revealing an unhurt skeleton. He stood there unfazed, his pale bones on display for all to see. Some of them had cracked from the heat, but they'd regenerated almost instantly.

"Kekeke. See? You finally understand now?"

"Well, I do understand that you're a complete dumbass."

"Huh?"

"Why don't you take a good look at yourself?"

Captain Roach obediently looked down at himself. There was a cursed cutlass in his hands and the white bones that made up his frame, but that was all.

"Aaaaaaaaaaaaaaaaaaaaaaah?!" Indeed, his coat, his hat, his shoes, and most importantly, his Light magic repelling cape had all been torched the flames. His shock was evident on his face. He looked more like a comical Halloween costume than a fearsome ghost pirate.

I started chanting slowly.

**"Come forth, O Light! Shining Exile:"**

"W-Wait! We can talk this out! I'll listen, so please don't. Don't—!"

**"[Banish]!"**

"Huhaughaue?!" My purifying Light magic reduced Captain Roach to dust.

His black cutlass fell to the deck with a metallic clang. I deftly picked it up and activated the Null spell, **[Power Rise].**

"Hiyah!" With my empowered arm, I split the sword in two and flung the pieces into the depths of the ocean. It didn't matter how rare an Artifact it was, I had no need for a cursed sword.

"Touya-dono, the fog is..." I looked up, and watched as the fog began to vanish. *So even the fog was part of that cutlass's curse.*

The gloomy clouds that had been hovering overhead cleared up as well. Sunlight poured down from the gaps in the clouds, its dazzling radiance illuminating the ocean.

"Looks like this sea's curse has been lifted."

"Most likely."

The curse that had plagued this sea for over a hundred years, claiming the lives of any crew unfortunate enough to sail into its waters, had finally been dispelled.

"I see. So the cutlass *was* cursed. Among Artifacts, there are those that use the life force of people to power themselves. That sword was probably one of them. Had we ignored it, it would have only continued to grow more dangerous." I was back in the garden's gazebo, listening to Cesca's explanation. Her description of it reminded me of those magical swords that fed on blood. Breaking it had been the right choice.

The jewel Yamamoto Kansukay had back in Eashen must have been something similar. Curses and the undead seemed to go hand in hand.

According to Cesca, some items had their curses woven into them as they were made, while others were normal items that were cursed later on.

"I believe there should have been a grimoire on curses in the Library of Babylon."

"Hey, don't just leave dangerous things like that lying around." So Doctor Babylon had been a dangerous person after all.

"If you want to break a curse, you have to start by learning how to make them. Plagues, banes, divine retribution… There's all sorts of curses out there. Come to think of it, I believe there's a curse out there capable of calling forth disaster too."

"A curse that can bring about disaster…"

*That sounds like one of those misfortune curses. Kind of like how there's people who are always hounded by bad luck. You know, the kind of people who always have bad things happen to them… Hm? Huh? Why's everyone staring at me?!*

"I see. A curse that brings disaster, you say... Or if you want to rephrase it, a curse that invites misfortune," Yumina replied.

"Why do I feel like you're all making fun of me?"

"Can such a curse be dispelled?"

*Hey, wait just a second. What are you all implying? That I'm under this disaster curse? Haha, don't make me laugh.*

"It's a shame he isn't aware of it..." The four girls all sighed at Elze's comment.

*Huh?* I glanced over at Kohaku, but the damn tiger just averted its gaze. *Hey now... It's not like I go out looking for trouble, all right? Trouble just always finds me... Yep. There's no way I'm cursed. No way at all... I think.*

I offered a small prayer up to God, just in case. Though I had no idea if that would be enough to free me from any such curse.

Hello there. Patora Fuyuhara here.

For no good reason, the third volume ended up being full of undead. Really, how did this happen?

I thought this when I finished the second volume too, but I can't believe we're at the third volume already.

I introduced a lot of characters that are going to become important in later volumes here. They probably won't have a chance to shine in the near future, but I'd be happy if you at least kept them in the back of your mind somewhere as you continue reading.

I'm sure most of you have guessed, but Eashen, which makes an appearance in this volume, was based off of Japan's Warring States Era. However, while some of the characters' names may resemble those of famous historical figures, there's no direct relation between them whatsoever. Sorry about that.

Oh yeah, I think I already mentioned this back in volume one, but I write this whole thing on my smartphone. Even when I pass the manuscript off to my editor, I check over everything on my smartphone. Plus, all of my submissions to the website, Shosetsuka ni Narou, were done on my phone as well. And when I stop for a break, I just play mobile games.

Honestly, staring at my smartphone all day puts a lot of strain on my eyes. I should probably look into getting some good eye drops. Or eat more blueberries. Though apparently studies on how antioxidants affect sight aren't conclusive... Too bad.

Alright, enough with the rambling and on to the acknowledgments.

I'd like to thank my illustrator, Eiji Usatsuka. Those swimsuits you drew for this volume's color pages were amazing. Thank you so much for all your hard work.

I'd also like to thank my editor, K. Thanks for putting up with all my phone calls. Sorry we always end up getting off topic...

And a big thanks to everyone at the Hobby Japan editorial department, along with everyone else who had a hand in the publication of this book. Without you, I would be nothing.

Last but not least, thank you to all of the readers on Shosetsuka ni Narou that gave my story a chance in the first place.

- Patora Fuyuhara

# J-Novel Club Lineup

## Ebook Releases Series List

Amagi Brilliant Park
An Archdemon's Dilemma: How to Love Your Elf Bride
Ao Oni
Arifureta Zero
Arifureta: From Commonplace to World's Strongest
Bluesteel Blasphemer
Brave Chronicle: The Ruinmaker
Clockwork Planet
Demon King Daimaou
Der Werwolf: The Annals of Veight
ECHO
From Truant to Anime Screenwriter: My Path to "Anohana" and "The Anthem of the Heart"
Gear Drive
Grimgar of Fantasy and Ash
How a Realist Hero Rebuilt the Kingdom
How NOT to Summon a Demon Lord
I Saved Too Many Girls and Caused the Apocalypse
If It's for My Daughter, I'd Even Defeat a Demon Lord
In Another World With My Smartphone
Infinite Dendrogram
Infinite Stratos
Invaders of the Rokujouma!?
JK Haru is a Sex Worker in Another World
Kokoro Connect
Last and First Idol
Lazy Dungeon Master
Me, a Genius? I Was Reborn into Another World and I Think They've Got the Wrong Idea!
Mixed Bathing in Another Dimension
My Big Sister Lives in a Fantasy World
My Little Sister Can Read Kanji
My Next Life as a Villainess: All Routes Lead to Doom!
Occultic;Nine
Outbreak Company
Paying to Win in a VRMMO
Seirei Gensouki: Spirit Chronicles
Sorcerous Stabber Orphen: The Wayward Journey
The Faraway Paladin
The Magic in this Other World is Too Far Behind!
The Master of Ragnarok & Blesser of Einherjar
The Unwanted Undead Adventurer
Walking My Second Path in Life
Yume Nikki: I Am Not in Your Dream